STORM DEATHS

Steve Orme

To Sue, Sean, Jo, Toby and Holly

1

She hated this man with the kind of hostility she usually reserved for former lovers. Yet she didn't even know him.

Her mind deviated to a holiday she'd had the previous summer in Greece and a sign outside a bar in Zakynthos which had made her chuckle: "our beer is as cold as your ex's heart". She considered whether this man actually had a heart.

She braced herself for the pain. That was what she expected whenever she saw him, although that hadn't been very often.

Every muscle in her body flinched as she tried to haul herself up. She was on an old-fashioned, single bed with a brass headboard which fitted in well with the surroundings. Retro, she thought – but not in a trendy way.

She didn't get far before her efforts were hampered by handcuffs which fixed her right arm firmly to the metal behind her. She recognised them as being similar to a pair she'd bought from an adult shop for her best friend's hen night. They were a constant source of amusement that evening; she wasn't laughing now.

Where was her mobile? She looked around but didn't even get a glimpse of her smartphone with its distinctive, multi-coloured case.

The man hovered over her. She was almost overcome by the smell of fatty food, cheap cigarettes and unwashed armpits. He undid a corner of the gaffa tape that covered her mouth, then yanked off the whole strip. She winced and closed her eyes, refusing to give him the satisfaction of seeing her cry.

When she opened them she saw again the red and gold floral wallpaper which must have gone out of fashion several decades ago and the curtains which despite their age refused to allow even a shaft of light to penetrate them. A single light bulb without a shade hung from the ceiling; prison couldn't be as bad as this, could it?

The only noise she heard was the rain hammering against the windowpane. She hated being out when it was wet and always made sure she had a coat and an umbrella at hand – even if the weather forecast suggested only an occasional light shower. How she wished she were out in the rain right now . . .

Who lives in a house like this, she wondered: a mummy's boy who never escaped his mother's clutches? A single man whose attempts to attract a woman were totally inadequate?

Her eyes opened wide as she recalled a similar property: the one her grandmother had lived in for sixty years. Her dear grandmother, a kind-hearted Christian who always put others before herself. Even to the extent that she refused to bother anybody when she was ill. Her grandmother who thought she would get better on her own. Her grandmother who'd been dead for two days before anyone found her.

It was the sort of house the woman wouldn't normally be seen dead in. She stiffened: would it be days before she was found dead, just like her grandmother?

2

The Mickleover to Etwall country path was a delight during the day. Its tranquillity and natural beauty offered an appealing break from the freneticism of the city suburb which had tried but failed to overwhelm it.

Whether the route was responsible for any frightening episodes at night wasn't generally known because so few people bothered to use it once daylight had faded.

It didn't bother Bob Fairfax. He knew there'd be no riders on the National Cycle Network Route 54 after dark: serious cyclists plotted their journeys days in advance and those who went on the occasional bike ride stayed away because there were no street lights to guide their way.

Bob used it simply because it was the quickest way home. He'd grown tired of the pubs in Mickleover and walked the three miles to Etwall where he felt the beer was better and the conversation too.

The trek back home wasn't too taxing for the former railway maintenance man. He was light on his feet despite just passing his seventieth birthday. Walking was his main form of exercise and with a few pints inside him he found he could go faster even if he had to be more careful because of the sodden leaves which at this time of year were falling freely from the trees.

Thankfully the rain that had caused meteorologists to issue flood warnings across the East Midlands had died down; if his clothes were wet by the time he arrived home it would be through sweat rather than showers.

He looked up. Only two days from a full moon and there was enough illumination to guide him, although the murky, gunmetal clouds had every intention of obliterating the light before Bob reached the first of several farm gates that blocked his way.

The only thing he'd heard for several minutes was the sound of his sturdy shoes grinding against the path's surface. But then a rustling in front of him caused him to frown. He peered into a gloomy, almost impenetrable hedge at one end of a field where cows usually spent their mind-numbingly tedious days.

Stupid old fool, Bob chided himself. Just a fox or some other animal that preferred this time of day.

He subconsciously pulled up the lapel of his thin coat as the wind gusted on his bare neck.

He set off again and had gone only a few yards when something glinted through a small gap where the moon penetrated ancient trees that hung over the path. He relaxed when he realised it was a bike, relatively new but abandoned because of a twisted front wheel.

As he walked on he recalled the heyday of the railway line. It used to be vital for the local community. But passenger services had stopped when he was a lad and freight trains had been phased out by the time he'd become a teenager.

Bob knew he'd soon come to a couple of bridges. One, Badger's Bridge, got its name because there were setts nearby. It reminded him of a fictional location in the television drama series *Midsomer Murders*.

He was approaching Heage Lane Bridge where in the past he'd seen copies of the New Testament and religious pamphlets left by Christians who were keen to share their faith. This time there was something else which seemed out of place.

As Bob walked on he realised it was a man slumped on a bench.

'You all right, mate?' Bob said, an opening line in a conversation which usually elicited a standard and not always truthful answer.

No reply. Not even an acknowledgement.

Stuff you, thought Bob. Manners cost nothing but if you can't be bothered to grunt out a reply, I'm not going to waste any more breath.

As Bob passed the bench, he noticed the man's head was nestling in his chest; he looked like someone who'd nodded off in front of the television.

Bob crouched down for a closer look – and saw the man wasn't breathing.

Trying to jump up and run off in the same movement, Bob fell backwards. He turned on one side and put his hand out to steady himself. He sat for a few moments, the dampness of the path turning his trousers a darker colour.

Think, you idiot, Bob chastised himself. What would a detective on one of those television series he was so fond of do in this situation?

He got to his feet. Looking around, he realised there was no one else nearby. Relief. Whoever had attacked this man was nowhere to be seen. Had he made a swift getaway? Or had this poor guy been here for some time with not even inquisitive wildlife to disturb him?

He pulled his antiquated mobile phone out of his jacket, composed himself and dialled 999.

3

Detective Inspector Miles Davies took an album out of its cover and slid it from its inner sleeve, holding it by its edge and centre without getting his fingerprints on the vinyl.

Tubular Bells by Mike Oldfield. Miles' father had bequeathed him his record collection when he died. Everything from avant-garde and trad jazz to blues, gospel, soul music and heavy rock.

The troubled genius that was Oldfield. The first release on the Virgin Records label and used on the soundtrack of *The Exorcist*. Music lauded as daring as well as experimental. Miles didn't care about its history; he just found it relaxing late-night listening.

He sat down with the latest edition of the East Midlands Express, bought at a nearby convenience store along with a ready meal which lay half-eaten on a well-used coffee table, milk and a box of cereal for the following morning's breakfast.

He scanned the usual reports of second-tier criminals being sent down for everything from fraud to assault before moving on to a story about a council's complaint that the government gave it "inadequate" funding.

He skipped over uninteresting, syndicated features which were in the paper only because they were cheap to buy rather than being intellectually stimulating.

When he turned to the sport, his curiosity was piqued by a headline right across one of the pages:

MYSTERY SURROUNDS STORM'S AMERICAN STAR

Written by Kevin Michaels, the story filled a spot usually reserved for the latest news from one of the region's football teams. The revelation that a player who'd made only a few first-team appearances had picked up a groin strain would make the lead on a quiet day – but here was something about the Derby Storm basketball club. With a headline like that, Davies thought, it won't be about anything they've achieved *on* the court.

'Allegations about Derby Storm's latest American import Yandel Eliot have emerged only a few weeks after the former Duke University player arrived in the city.

There are reports that police wanted to speak to him about the murder of a friend who was stabbed to death after visiting a nightclub in Durham, North Carolina.

Storm management have remained tight-lipped about the speculation. We have tried to reach the 6ft 10in centre for comment.

But Storm fans have been asking why a player of Eliot's calibre is playing in Derby. He averaged an impressive 12 points and 11 rebounds in his senior year at Duke and there was a surprise when he did not put himself forward for the world's greatest league, the NBA.

He was then expected to sign for a top European club where he could command a six-figure salary.

But whether he could not take the pressure of playing at such a high level or if there is a secret behind Eliot's appearance in Derby remains to be seen.

For now, Storm supporters are basking in the quality and flair that Eliot brings to the team. The question on all their lips, though, is: will he still be here at the end of the season?'

Davies re-read the report, trying to think of a reason why Eliot would choose to come to Derby. He must have had the right papers and he wouldn't have a criminal record or he wouldn't get a work permit to play in this country.

Davies made a mental note to check for any comments on social media. He was determined to see what else he could find out about Yandel Eliot.

He was startled as his phone rang. He groaned, not because he knew he would have to go back to work but because he'd get little sleep tonight.

'DI Davies.'

'Sorry to bother you, sir. I know you're not on call but we're struggling at the moment. The on-call detective inspector's already dealing with one major incident and now we've got a body. This one's near your home, so can you deal with it?'

4

Davies swung his car out of a side street onto Station Approach in Derby and headed towards the crime scene. The roads were quiet at that time of night: a few drinkers spilling out of a pub, some with so much alcohol in them they needed a greasy kebab to settle their stomach, others waiting in high spirits for a taxi to take them home.

Within minutes the detective inspector was on the A516 heading for Etwall, a village he knew only because of its secondary school, which had an inordinate number of pupils, and its annual well dressing festival – an obscure English tradition in which wooden frames are lavishly decorated with flower petals to offer thanks for the water supply.

Davies knew the cycle path vaguely – he'd walked down part of it once when someone suggested off-duty officers should take part in a weekend ramble. Getting to it by car had proved problematic.

Driving past an auction house and the site of a disused farm which used to pride itself on the happiness of its hens, he eventually saw a number of police vehicles parked near a bridge.

A forensic team was already there, erecting lights and two white tents, one to aid their investigation, the other to hide the body from any prying eyes. Not that anybody was in the area at that time of night.

Davies pulled on a face mask, a pair of gloves, a white over-suit with a hood, overshoes and a second pair of gloves. With any investigation he was eager to get a good look at the crime scene himself; photos didn't always give the right perspective or tell him everything he might want to know.

Detective Sergeant James West, looking drained despite most of his stocky frame being covered up by his personal protective equipment, strode towards Davies.

'Had a good couple of days off, James?'

'Yeah, not bad, thanks.'

'Pity you couldn't find time to have a shave.'

West grinned. His boss was a stickler for convention; he didn't want the public to have any reason to criticise his team for not looking the part. But at this time of day Davies didn't expect his officers to be dressed up as if they were having an audience with the Queen.

'What have we got?' The adrenaline was flowing through Davies' body and the gusting wind was playing its part in keeping him alert.

'White male, probably early to late fifties. Somebody's given him a good beating.'

'So how did he get from the road onto the path? A good fifty yards or more, so d'you reckon we're looking for a group of people, a gang maybe?'

'Either that or someone who's really strong. Bodybuilder?'

Davies hesitated while he thought about some of the criminals he knew who'd be capable of murder and who could plan what appeared to be a less-than-straightforward attack.

'Must have had a car. There's no way anyone, not even a gang, would want to carry him from Etwall or Mickleover. Either they had a vehicle or it's someone living fairly close. There don't seem to be many houses nearby.

'Is there a cordon in place?'

'We've got an inner cordon sorted, boss. First thing we did.'

'What about an outer cordon?'

'Someone's checking it out now. There's access from the path that you can see, just up there – apart from that, the nearest paths are about a mile in each direction. We're getting them sealed off now.'

Davies looked both ways but could see little through the gloom as rain started falling again.

'Who found the body?'

'Guy over there. Walking back from the pub.'

Davies was taken aback. He didn't expect anyone to be walking home on a dark path without any lighting. That wasn't a crime – but was the man capable of murder? Had he killed the man on the bench and claimed he'd just found him on his way home?

'Any idea of a motive?'

'Well, boss, we found the guy's wallet on the floor. Don't worry – I was very careful. Haven't contaminated anything. He's got money on him, he's still got his watch and mobile phone, so it doesn't look as if it was robbery.

'Inside his wallet I could see a card. National Union of Journalists. There's probably no shortage of people who wanted to have a go at him.'

'Why's that?'

'He's Kevin Michaels, journalist on the local newspaper. You know what Donald Trump called reporters? The most dishonest human beings on earth. I bet Michaels has been responsible for a fair amount of fake news.'

Davies bristled. 'Don't forget, James, that Kevin Michaels was somebody's son. Could have been married with kids. Someone will miss him. Even hard-hearted colleagues – they'll probably be devastated. He's no different to any other victim. We've got to make sure we get justice for his family, friends.'

West looked down as though he were searching for evidence.

Davies recalled the article in the Express written by Michaels about the Derby Storm player Yandel Eliot. Maybe he was jumping to conclusions but could Eliot have anything to do with Michaels' death?

'Anything else?'

'I think the killer wanted to send out a message.'

'What makes you think that, James?'

'Michaels has got a fountain pen sticking out of his chest.'

5

The pounding, persistent overnight rain had stopped and the sun was making a determined attempt to brighten up what threatened to be a depressing day. But another black, ominous cloud was preparing to tip its contents on the city. Umbrella salespeople were again anticipating good business.

Ken Thompson swaggered as he strode down the street. At six feet six inches tall and with a toned physique that a professional athlete would be proud of, Thompson knew he was an imposing sight. But many people looked up to him because of his kindness and generosity; they regarded him as a gentle giant.

His grey hair, not as thick as he would like at the temples but still long enough for him to wear in a ponytail, gave him the appearance of an ageing rock star. It just about covered his ears which stuck out at an angle that some people would find embarrassing. But the last person who'd poked fun at them ended up in the accident and emergency department of the nearest hospital and Thompson had been expelled from school.

People who didn't know him found him threatening because of his shadowy eyes which seemed to bore right into their soul and the scar on his right cheek. That was a permanent reminder of a battle he'd won when a young upstart tried to muscle in on his empire.

Yet those who relied on him whenever they fell on hard times wouldn't believe he had a bad gene in his body.

The residents of a run-down Nottingham sink estate had Thompson to thank for making the community comfortable in their surroundings. He would provide anyone who had trouble finding the money for food or a utility bill with a financial lifeline – and he didn't expect repayment. He knew the date of everyone's birthday; the women always received an extravagant bouquet of flowers while the men were given beer or spirits and, if they smoked, cigars.

This morning the streets were quiet; those who had jobs had already left for work, the considerable number who were unemployed had no reason to leave their beds on what was an overcast, soulless morning.

Thompson's gaze fell on a woman dressed in an ill-fitting tracksuit whose grey, lined face gave her the look of a woman in her sixties. She'd recently clocked up her forty-fifth birthday.

He spoke in a soft, concerned voice: 'Anything wrong, Julie?'

Thompson knew Julie Mason and her family. Her husband had disappeared with a younger woman and left her to look after their two children. She'd made a commendable job of it and never took up with another man.

20

'Oh, Ken, we're in such a mess . . .' Her sobs prevented him from hearing anything else she said. Thompson put his arm around her shoulder as tears glistened on her cheeks and dripped onto her top.

She explained that her five-year-old grandson Ethan had been diagnosed with neuroblastoma – the most common cancer in children. He was at stage L2: the cancer hadn't spread but it couldn't be removed safely by surgery. The National Health Service wanted Ethan to be part of a clinical trial to assess the effectiveness of different treatments – but it was refusing to pay for drugs which had no licence for use in the UK.

'You can get those drugs in America. I'd do anything for Ethan but I just can't afford the money for him to go there. I'm at my wits' end,' she wailed.

'Where's Ethan now?'

'He's at home. He's been in hospital but there's not a lot they can do for him. Me and the daughter can look after him and he's better in his own bed with his toys around him. But he's going to get worse. I just don't know what to do.'

Thompson tightened his grip on her shoulder and pulled her in close.

'Here's what I want you to do. Go home, put the kettle on, have a cup of tea and try not to worry. I know that won't be easy, but leave it to me. I'll make a few phone calls, see what I can sort out. But there's one thing you shouldn't do.'

'What's that?'

'Give up hope.'

6

Felicity Strutt had the reputation of being a very good weather forecaster. But she failed to predict how her manner and loftiness made her unpopular with some of her colleagues. When she failed to turn up for work one morning there was a mixture of genuine concern for her but also an indifferent attitude from those who'd never liked her from the first moment they'd set eyes on her.

The previous day had gone really well and her appearance on the regional television news was flawless. No stumbles and a perfect delivery. This was despite being told only moments before she went on air that the programme was overrunning and she had to cut thirty seconds from her allotted time.

'Thank you very much, everyone. Well done, Felicity,' the director had said. Sweat trickled down his face and back as the stress of handling the live, technically complicated show had almost got the better of him.

He relaxed as draughts of cool air washed over him in the stilted, unnatural, dimly lit room which transmitted the programme each evening.

Felicity had declined the offer of drinks after the show and left on her own.

Ten minutes later a group of her colleagues found themselves in a classy, up-market wine bar within walking distance of the office. Copies of famous paintings adorned the brick walls; chairs had been chosen to fit in with the ambience rather than for their comfort. It was a place people frequented to make an impression. Entrepreneurs, business associates and company bosses were vying for attention, boasting that theirs had been the biggest deal of the week if not the year.

The conversation soon turned to the television station's star forecaster.

'Who does she think she is?' the director groaned, his Yorkshire accent making the remark sound all the more threatening. 'She presents the weather. She's not our chief news reporter. Strutting about the newsroom. Lives up to her name, she does. And have you seen her when she puts her hair in curls? Looks like Little Bo Peep.'

'Why didn't she join us? Did she actually say she was meeting a contact?' asked a technical operator who'd have preferred a glass of real ale in front of him.

'That's what she told me. She'll want to present the programme next!'

'Let's give her the benefit of the doubt. She wouldn't be the first to go from presenting the weather to reading the news,' said a PA who'd never criticised anyone in her life.

'She's well in with the management. The other day I heard the editor arranging to take her for a meal,' grumbled a correspondent who'd never even got a drink out of his boss.

'It's her husband I feel sorry for.' The picture editor was already well into his second glass of red. 'Don't know what he sees in her. Don't know how he puts up with her. She can be a real nightmare to work with.'

A camera operator jumped to her defence. 'Leave her alone. Whenever I'm out on location with her, she's a real pro. Can be too much of a perfectionist. She might want to do a piece to camera several times, but it's for the good of the programme. What about the awards we've won recently? She played a big part. And nobody knows more about coffee shops in this area than she does – she must have been in all of them!'

'She only does it to make her CV look better,' the picture editor whined. 'And her showreel. She'll be off to bigger and better things before too long. We'll be the ones who helped her to get there.'

Felicity Strutt had divided opinion from the first day she joined the station two years previously. Slender, with long, blonde hair that not even the strongest wind could blow out of place, she always looked immaculate. She had an unfortunate trait: her nose was angled slightly upwards. It made her the type of person that people loved or hated.

Men fancied her or thought she was haughty; women warmed to her or simply didn't trust her.

Colleagues either admired her for her ambition and her intrinsic desire to make the most of her talents or thought she was too big for her boots.

'I couldn't care less what she gets up to outside work.' The director adopted a much sterner tone – it wasn't the wine speaking. 'If she tries to interfere with any of my programmes, there'll be trouble.'

7

Rob Woodcock paced around the living room floor, the beginnings of a furrow appearing in the carpet. Where the hell was Felicity?

He'd called her mobile phone countless times but he heard only her automated message. He'd texted her on a regular basis but didn't hear the reassuring 'ping' to signal that his wife had replied.

He knew he ought to have shown a little more interest the previous day when she revealed she'd arranged to meet someone after work. But he was preoccupied with a presentation to a major client which could earn the PR company he worked for a huge sum of money. Shit! Why hadn't he listened to her?

He rubbed his hand through his hair and scratched underneath his chin where the best part of two days' growth was visible.

He'd rung everyone he could think of to try to locate her. Friends, colleagues, even her boss. But no, they hadn't seen her, they didn't know who she was meeting and she hadn't stayed the night with them.

He lit another cigarette. Felicity always insisted he went outside to smoke and badgered him endlessly about giving up. But his stress levels were off the scale; he'd go out of his mind without something to calm him down, even if it worked only momentarily. Right now he'd love to hear Felicity's voice chastising him for lighting up in the house. But he heard nothing.

He looked up the numbers of hospitals within a twenty-mile radius. Each one gave him the same answer: no one with the name of Felicity Strutt or Woodcock had been admitted. No accident, no illness, no patient.

After more phone calls which proved fruitless, he grabbed his coat and left the flat.

The Central Police Station in Byron House at the top of Maid Marian Way had escaped a cull of police stations mainly because of a decision by the former chief constable to restructure the Nottinghamshire force geographically. It was prompted by a huge rise in knife crime which was considered a national epidemic.

A superintendent had been appointed to run the city division and ensure that the police were seen to be responding to a conundrum that was destroying the lives of young and old alike. Even children as young as six had been caught taking knives into school; teachers, parents and grandparents were all alarmed that society was unable to find a remedy.

Apart from that, Byron House had been operational only since 2016 when the police station was opened by Prince Harry, the Duke of Sussex, on one of his regular visits to the city.

Rob Woodcock walked through the double glass doors into an area which reminded him of a doctor's surgery or a pharmacy. The clinical atmosphere was heightened by chairs in lines where people were expected to sit before they were called to the counter.

Woodcock took in everything around him, his leg twitching as his fears about Felicity grew more acute. TV monitors spelled out messages about community protection, compliments from people who'd received a good service and the police's PROUD values – being Professional, having Respect for all, working together in One team, demonstrating the Utmost integrity, trust and honesty, and Doing it differently.

There was a plaque as a tribute to Ged Walker, a police dog handler killed in the line of duty in 2003. What a legacy, Woodcock thought. You give up your life in your job and all you get is a plaque on a wall that few people see.

The enquiry officer sighed. Only a couple of hours into his shift and already his eyelids were drooping. His shoulders sagged and his frown would have been more appropriate at a funeral.

He was struggling to stay awake. He had a stomach-tightening sickness, the sort of feeling he experienced when he had to get up in the early hours for a flight to a continental destination for a fortnight's break. But this was no holiday . . .

More than likely another boring shift was in store, with only the occasional shot of caffeine to keep him going. That was if one of his colleagues managed to find the time to get him a drink.

When he first joined the front counter staff he loved everything about the job: looking after victims and witnesses, taking routine statements, the general banter with officers. But so much had changed. Everyone was so busy they rarely had time for a chat. The police station looked pristine and pure but it couldn't hide the stench of stale beer from drunks who'd spent a night in the cells.

He hardly noticed the small, haggard-looking man with fear in his eyes who stood bolt upright just a few feet away from him.

'Can I help you, sir?'

'Yes. I've come to report a missing person.'

'And what is the person's name?'

'Felicity. Felicity Strutt. She's my wife. That's her professional name. Her married name is Woodcock.'

The enquiry officer reached below the counter for a pad so that he could make notes.

'Why do you think she's missing?'

'She left work shortly after seven yesterday evening. Said she was meeting a business associate. I've not heard from her since. She never stays out at night. It's just not like her. Always lets me know where she's going, what she's doing. But she's not answering her phone and she hasn't replied to my texts. I'm worried that something's happened to her.'

The man took down details of Felicity's age, address, telephone numbers, height and distinctive features.

'Any health problems?'

'No. She takes pride in being healthy and keeping fit.'

'Is she on any medication?'

'No, none.'

'Have you got a photograph of her?'

Woodcock pulled out of his pocket a recent publicity shot which had the television station's name emblazoned across the bottom.

'Oh, now I know who she is! I've seen her on the box, on the evening news. On the odd occasion when I can watch it. If I'm on afternoons I've no chance. When I'm on earlies, sometimes I fall asleep as soon as the programme comes on. I haven't seen it for a couple of days – the kids always want to watch Netflix.'

'Will you please take this seriously? She didn't come home last night and I'm certain something's happened to her.'

'I can assure you, sir, I *am* taking this seriously. However, she's a normal, healthy person. There might be a perfectly valid reason why she hasn't been in touch. But we'll set the wheels in motion and see if we can find her.'

'What does that involve?'

'I'll make out a report for my sergeant. Her details will be circulated to all our operational officers. They'll also be sent to other forces in the UK and internationally. We'll feature her disappearance on our social media channels. If she wants to be found, I'm sure we'll locate her.'

Woodcock spluttered, his face becoming redder as he took a step closer to the counter.

'What do you mean, *if* she wants to be found?'

'Sir, do you realise how many people go missing? In Britain over eight hundred people are recorded as missing every day. Some people don't want the police or other agencies to disclose where they are. If that's the case, we have to keep their details confidential.'

'I'm not concerned about other people. I just know that this is completely out of character for Felicity.'

'In that case, sir, you can help us by drawing up a list of her associates, places she visits on a regular basis, that sort of thing. Is that all right?'

Woodcock gulped before continuing.

'I'll do anything – anything to find her.'

The enquiry officer looked through a check list of actions the police had to run through whenever anyone reported a missing person.

'What was she wearing the last time you saw her?'

Woodcock looked down, embarrassed.

'I, I can't remember. I was tied up when she left for work. I should have taken more notice.'

'Not to worry. I'm sure some of her colleagues can tell us. At some stage we may need a DNA sample. Will that be okay?'

'Of course.'

'How about publicity? Sometimes that can help to generate new leads. I'm sure you won't have any objection to that.'

'That's fine.'

'We also need permission to approach her doctor and dentist for her medical and dental records.'

'You've got it.'

'Thank you very much, sir. You've been very co-operative. One last thing: does she have a car?'

'Yes. As far as I know, she was driving it when she left work.'

'What make is it?'

'It's a Mercedes. Cabriolet. You know, a convertible. Although she rarely has the top down. Especially in this weather. Says it blows her hair about too much.'

'And the colour?'

'Bright red. You can see it coming a mile off.'

Feet apart, Woodcock gripped the counter with both hands.

'Right, I've done my bit. Now, what are you going to do about finding her?'

'Well, we'll start the ball rolling by checking where she was last seen. We'll check our ANPR cameras, see if we can spot her after she left work. Phone records – we'll find out who she was talking to, see if that gives us any clues. We'll get onto it as soon as we can.'

'But why wait? Why aren't you launching a full-scale search now? She could be in real danger. Some nutter who's seen her on the telly could have abducted her   or worse.'

'I understand your concern, sir – '

'Do you? Do you really?'

'This must be very stressful for you but, as I said earlier, there's probably a perfectly valid reason why she hasn't been in touch.'

Woodcock skulked out of the police station. An empty beer can had been left on the pavement right in front of him. He lashed out; it shot down the road, almost hitting an elderly woman with a walking stick.

'What was that all about?' A senior detective poked his head around the door at the end of the police station counter.

The enquiry officer chuckled. 'Just some bloke who wanted to report his wife missing. She went out for the night and hasn't come home. Probably shagging one of his mates somewhere.'

8

The headquarters of the East Midlands Constabulary was a technological marvel, a twenty-million-pound building on the southern edge of the city which police and crime commissioners from all over the country looked at with envy.

The building was designed to meet the challenges of modern-day policing. It didn't please conservationists who thought the huge number of solar panels it boasted were a particularly unattractive feature – but they meant there was no need for central heating and running costs were cheap. In fact they were far cheaper than the separate offices used by police forces in Nottinghamshire, Leicestershire and Derbyshire before their amalgamation.

The new building's gloss, though, couldn't disguise the fact that fewer people wanted to go there to report a crime. Although it was well served by public transport, including the tram, it was too far out of the centre to encourage use by the public.

Those at the top of the force had closed a number of provincial police stations, using research which showed that people tended to ring 101 rather than make a personal visit. But the move had proved controversial, with some businesses accusing the police of withdrawing from areas of high crime in the city.

The opening of the headquarters and the merger also coincided with a swingeing cut in the number of officers employed by the force. The swanky, ten-storey building housed seven-hundred officers working across all departments in open-plan offices which encouraged collaboration. Most of one floor was taken up with the department looking after one of the force's strategic priorities: cybercrime. But it meant fewer officers could get out onto the streets and meet the public; community policing had noticeably suffered despite the attempts of senior management to categorise people above buildings.

In the room dubbed Robert Peel which was used as the base for most major incidents, Davies called for order. Scores of officers paid attention straightaway. He could feel a definite buzz, an electrifying aura that was always evident at the start of a major investigation.

'Good morning everyone. Phones off or on silent, please. Okay, James, bring us up to date.'

West had already loaded up a state-of-the-art laptop with basic details of the investigation. A photograph appeared on a screen which took up a whole wall of the incident room.

He was like a seasoned public speaker, confidently telling his colleagues what was known so far and only occasionally having to look down at his notes.

'Kevin Michaels, fifty-two-years-old, journalist. Married with two kids, boy and a girl. They're in secondary schools in Derby.

35

According to his news editor, Michaels was a hard-working, reliable reporter who never took any risks, never went too far when reporting a story. Could have gone to work for a national paper but didn't want to uproot the kids. Might have upset a few criminals by covering their court cases, otherwise he didn't appear to have any enemies.'

'Thanks, James. Let's do all the usual checks, find out as much about him as we can. Is there CCTV near the crime scene? It's an isolated spot but there are a few places nearby that might have their own cameras. Let's get hold of any footage. What about Michaels' bank account? Find out if there've been any unusual transactions. Mobile phone – who's he been talking to? Who wanted him dead? He must have upset someone for them to bump him off. Okay, let's get cracking.'

Davies was just about to leave the incident room when his boss, Detective Superintendent Keith Holland, confronted him. His suit, with a thin yet distinctive pinstripe, looked expensive; his dazzling shirt and tie dripped with quality and his shoes resembled an old-time police officer's footwear: you could see your face in them. He reeked of aftershave, a heady fragrance that was as overpowering as it was overpriced.

'Ah, Miles.' He sounded smug; his clipped tone was only one of the reasons why the lower ranks didn't give him respect.

With a solid, award-filled business background, he'd been parachuted into the force without having to undertake the long slog that characterised so many of his staff. Not for him pounding the streets, talking to ordinary people, sorting out the mayhem and terror that were the typical conclusions of alcohol-soaked weekends in a city centre. He'd been on a fast-track scheme which recognised his qualities as a leader – even though his man-management skills were virtually non-existent. Usually junior officers didn't mind outsiders taking top positions because they would immerse themselves in the strategies and office politics that no one else wanted to tackle. But Holland also wanted to play a major part in active investigations.

'Here's an interesting one for you. Missing person. Felicity Strutt, weather presenter on the local TV station's disappeared. Last sighting of her just after seven yesterday evening. Husband reported her missing. No sign of her since.'

Davies flinched. 'You're not suggesting we take that on as well? We had enough to keep us going for months before Kevin Michaels was murdered. Don't tell me – the police and crime commissioner wants to improve clear-up rates. That wouldn't have anything to do with his campaign for re-election in a few months, would it, sir?'

Holland brushed the remark aside. 'Of course I'm not giving you that as well. Uniform are perfectly capable of looking after it. Just keep an eye on it. It might be a bit far-fetched but Felicity's disappearance and Michaels' death might be linked. After all, they're in the same business.'

Davies turned his back on Holland and shook his head.

Holland resumed: 'The Chief Constable and I are together on this. There'll be a lot of public interest in the case; it's getting big on social media and there's a feeling it'll get a mention on the national news.'

Blood rushed to Davies' cheeks. Detective Superintendent Holland never failed to bring the Chief Constable's name into a conversation if he could. Holland was the type who did as little work as possible yet took maximum credit. Nor was he quick to hand out plaudits when they were due. He believed officers on the front line got job satisfaction; they didn't need his praise as well.

'We'll set up a press conference fairly soon. From what I gather, Felicity's very popular. The public love her. I'm sure they'll want to help.'

And I'm sure your face will be all over the television, Davies thought. Holland would want the exposure to show chief constables across the UK how adept he was at handling a major investigation. But he wouldn't be the one who'd have to go through all the calls from people wanting to say how sorry they were that the 'lovely' weather forecaster had gone missing or thought they'd seen her in Yorkshire, Cornwall or Kent.

Holland turned to go but stopped in the doorway. 'Oh, a couple of other things. Any success on those disturbances in the student area?'

'We've got a few young scrotes in custody. Questioning them later.'

'And that big punch-up in the nightclub last weekend?'

'We're getting there. But it's taking time to interview all the witnesses, trying to piece together what it was really about. We could move quicker if we'd got more officers working on it.'

Holland's eyes glazed over, the disdain evident in his voice. 'Well, you know that's not going to happen because the police and crime commissioner's stopped overtime. He's saved millions so far. I can't believe how much duplication there was across the three forces.

'And what about that prowler – the man in the mask, reported by the old woman who lives near the university?'

'Case solved,' said Davies, a smirk appearing on one side of his mouth.

'That was quick work. Where is he – in the cells?'

'Not exactly,' Davies offered.

'Well, where, then? Come on, man, spit it out!'

Davies paused like a game show host keeping a contestant in suspense just before the director goes to a commercial break. 'You may find it difficult to believe but the man we were looking for wasn't an intruder – he was wearing an elephant onesie. Going to a fancy-dress party. We sent a patrol to the scene – no crime, no arrest. The officers suggested we should call in the fashion police instead! Oh, they did have a friendly word with the dear old lady. Suggested she went to see an optician . . .'

9

Accompanied by West, Davies drove back along the A52 to Derby. The road was still busy even though the early-morning commuters had arrived at their places of work and parents had dropped off their precious children at school.

Davies knew parts of Oakwood, but as the suburb on the outskirts of the city was one of the largest new-housing estates in Europe, he didn't think twice about putting Kevin Michaels' address into his satnav.

He pulled up outside a four-bedroomed semi-detached house which was built in the 1980s and looked as though it had had little maintenance since then.

A small front lawn was overgrown and a hedge was crying out for a trim. The door and windows needed a coat of paint; the property had a tired rather than neglected look. Davies was under the impression that it was home to a busy family who had greater priorities than DIY.

The family liaison officer opened the door and led the two detectives into a compact living room. Clothes waiting to be ironed were scattered around along with toys and newspapers. Davies noticed several photographs of a young boy and girl, on the mantelpiece, on a shelf by the window and above a fireplace where a canvas print took up most of the wall. A couple of small table lamps only partially eradicated the darkness which spilled into the room from threatening black skies.

Helen Michaels was sitting hunched up on a well-worn armchair. She was younger than her husband but looked older. She was wearing a tightly tied dressing gown over a nightdress and slippers. Her hair drooped over one side of her face and her eyes were a vivid red; a tear was slowly making its way down her left cheek but she seemed not to care.

Davies had seen grief express itself in many ways. Some people acted as though nothing had happened; their actions didn't necessarily involve culpability. Others accepted the death of a loved one with stoicism and it might be a couple of weeks before the effects of a tragedy struck home.

It hadn't taken Helen Michaels long to realise that a huge part of her life had been taken from her.

The detective inspector sympathised with her for her loss, hoping his concern sounded genuine.

'I know it's not a good time, but I need to ask you a few questions about Kevin.'

Helen nodded but kept her eyes fixed on a spot on the carpet which needed cleaning.

'Do you know why he went out last night?'

Helen exhaled, puffing out her cheeks before she spoke.

'He said he was going to meet a few of the lads from work. They're so busy these days and most of them work in Nottingham, so they rarely get time for a drink. They were just having a couple of pints for a change.'

Another tear fell onto her other cheek.

'Any idea where they might have gone?'

'He didn't say. He usually goes to one that serves real ale. He can't abide these big pub chains that don't look after their beer.'

Davies noticed how Helen spoke about Michaels in the present tense. He couldn't begin to imagine what she was going through.

'Kevin's older than you, is that right?'

'Just over ten years older.'

Without prompting she recalled the early days of their relationship. 'When we met he was really involved in the union, the NUJ. Wanted to fight everyone's battles. But then he changed. Kept up his union membership but hardly went to any meetings. Said he couldn't be bothered with it any more.'

Davies tried to be as gentle as possible with Helen. 'How would you describe Kevin?'

'He's a good man. A loving husband, wonderful father. Loves his work but his family always comes first. And of course basketball. He couldn't believe it when the paper told him he could report on the Storm as well as doing his normal job. He'd take us all along to the games. Wants to show everyone what a happy family we are.'

She started sobbing continuously. Davies knew he wouldn't get much more out of her so he nodded to West and they got up to leave.

'Who would do this to him? He'd never hurt anyone.' Helen Michaels shook her head as she gasped for breath. She cried with more anguish than a baby who'd been waiting hours to be fed.

Outside the house Davies walked onto the street with the highly experienced family liaison officer. He made sure no one was within earshot.

'Well, could she have done it?'

'I've not been in her company very long but I don't think I've ever seen anyone show so much grief over the death of a partner. There's no way you can put that on. I know a large percentage of murder victims know their killer, but there's no way Helen Michaels could have killed her husband."

10

Yandel Eliot swung his size 16 feet off his extra-long bed onto the wooden floor and put his elbows on his knees. On the other side of the modern, luxuriously appointed bedroom his alarm clock was buzzing loudly and vibrating. He had to get up to switch it off; he resisted the urge to hurl it out of the window and lie down again.

Shuffling his feet towards the kitchen, he stooped so that he didn't hit his head on the door frame. He didn't do it consciously; there was something inside him that warned him his body was just too big for normal houses.

He appreciated the accommodation the Storm had provided for him. An executive, second-floor apartment in one of the better suburbs, it was comfortable, well-equipped, had all the television channels he could wish for and was convenient for the city centre. But he thought that if the basketball authorities in England were serious about taking the game to the next level, they ought to consider the needs of people like himself.

After all, he'd represented his college in a game at Madison Square Garden in New York – hardly anyone else who was playing in

England could say that. He loved the Garden's huge dressing rooms with their bigger-than-average doors which meant he didn't have to bend over like an old man. In the States they knew how to treat their assets properly.

His mobile phone pinged. A text from teammate Rick Parker who'd be with him in fifteen minutes. Eliot had just enough time for a coffee.

Eliot didn't like driving. He found it incomprehensible that in England you drove on the other side of the road. That was as baffling as finding your way around the streets. He'd never understood why English cities weren't divided into blocks.

He switched on the coffee machine before hauling himself off to the bathroom. He had to kneel in front of the basin to get low enough to splash his face, the water's cold edge only slightly making inroads into his lethargy.

He looked up and saw in the mirror his bloodshot eyes, dilated pupils and sallow complexion. His cheek muscle twitched. He slapped himself but the tic continued.

'Shit! I must have coffee before Rick gets here.'

He stared into space and watched a tiny spider crawling up the wall towards the shower head.

'Why's Rick coming here?' he said aloud, his mind struggling to focus on the day ahead.

He felt his stomach drop as if an opponent had dunked on him in the last second of a championship game. 'Practice! We're practising this morning! Where's my kit? Where did I leave it?'

He was still rushing around in a panic when the sound of the doorbell notched up his agitation even further.

Detective Superintendent Holland brushed past West in his eagerness to impress Davies. Holland's officious look was for once missing, replaced by a huge grin that made him look more pompous than ever.

'Miles. This is Tilly Johnson. Newly qualified DC. She's just moved here from Norfolk. You said you wanted more people on your team – she'll be with you for the foreseeable future. I know you'll take good care of her.'

Tilly Johnson's round face gave her a cute look which was reinforced by dimples that made her appear younger than she actually was. Her brown hair was swept off her face and tied in a ponytail, accentuating her striking features. But the first thing anyone noticed was her vivid blue eyes which had a hint of resilience as well as gentleness.

'Welcome along, Tilly. You're just in time for the morning briefing.'

West inched his way into the incident room, his eyes closing for longer than usual as he blinked.

He was wearing a suit, light blue shirt and patterned tie hanging loosely around his neck. Normally he looked the part but this morning it appeared as though someone had thrown a random set of clothes at him and somehow they'd managed to fit.

West had joined the police almost by accident. He left school with decent qualifications but didn't want to go to university or take up an apprenticeship. He moved from job to job without finding out what he was good at.

One Saturday morning he was in town with a few friends when he came across a noisy demonstration organised by an extreme left-wing group. It threatened to get violent until a line of police officers, well disciplined and working as a team, restored order. They arrested a couple of troublemakers who'd infiltrated the protest and marched them away.

West was so impressed that he went to the nearest police station and asked how he could join up.

He made solid progress and then trained to be a detective, his enthusiasm and hard work making up for his lack of common sense.

'You're looking a bit tired, James. Can't you stand the pace?' Davies asked.

He took the health of his staff seriously; the long, sometimes laborious hours could take their toll and he realised officers couldn't contribute to an investigation if they were exhausted.

'Sorry, boss. The new season of *The Tenth Kingdom*'s just come out. Watched several episodes last night. Think I might have watched one too many.'

'Don't know what you see in that fantasy stuff. I have enough problems with reality.'

West looked offended. 'It's one of the greatest series ever made. Can't believe you're not watching it.'

Davies recalled his only encounter with the genre. 'A couple of years ago I went to see something by Terry Pratchett. At the Lace Market Theatre. What was it? *Wyrd Sisters*. A rip-off of Shakespeare's *Macbeth* and several other plays too. That's a couple of hours of my life that I'll never get back. Couldn't understand it at all. Especially the bit about it being set in another world on the backs of four elephants which are riding a giant turtle. Mind-boggling.'

'That's *Discworld*,' West enthused. 'Did you know that Terry Pratchett wrote forty-one novels in the series? I'm trying to get through all of them.'

Davies shook his head. He had a lot of time for West: he'd come up through the ranks the traditional way, starting at the bottom and learning the old-fashioned methods that might seem boring at the time but were essential to solve a case. Not like the newer brand of detective, a graduate who went through a twelve-week, crash course that couldn't possibly produce an effective officer.

Davies had to admit that some of the newer recruits were quick on the uptake when they received their digital training; they were soon snapped up to help with offences like online abuse and cybercrime. But whenever some of the new-style investigators joined Davies' team, someone had to explain even the most elementary methods of producing evidence which would lead to an arrest.

He asked Paul Allen, a jovial DC who saw the funny side of most situations, to bring the team up to date with the latest findings.

'Here's what we've got on the deceased. Kevin Michaels, no police record – just the odd parking ticket. On the night he died he went for a drink with some of his colleagues from the East Midlands Express. The Smithfield, near the old Derby Telegraph building.'

Davies held up his hand to stop Allen.

'James and I will go to the newspaper after the meeting to find out who he met. Then I'll need someone to talk to the landlord and his staff. They might have had a late night but get them out of bed if necessary. They could potentially be suspects. And check for CCTV. They're bound to have it – let's hope it was working.

'Next, phone records, Mark, will you get hold of them?'

Mark Roberts, a dependable, enthusiastic detective who was a regular on Davies' team, nodded.

Allen resumed: 'We're waiting for DNA results. Hopefully we'll have them by this evening.'

Davies nodded his appreciation. 'Moving on, we're also keeping an eye on the disappearance of Felicity Strutt. You may know her as a weather forecaster on the local TV station. There might be a link to Kevin Michaels' murder, there might not. At this stage all we know is that she's been reported missing. Uniform are handling it but we need to keep across it in case it turns into an abduction.

49

'Okay, thanks, everyone. We'll see what we've got by midday and we might have another briefing then. Otherwise, we'll see you this afternoon for an update.'

Davies beckoned Tilly to join them as they left the police station and headed for the East Midlands Express.

The newspaper's offices were nothing unusual. In fact the building would have been ideal for solicitors, accountants or any commercial services company.

The Express no longer printed its own editions so it had no need for huge premises. Gone was the smell of hot metal, the heat generated by the presses as they worked to maximum capacity, and the inky feel of the papers; deadline day had taken on a new meaning.

Not that most of the staff of the East Midlands Express had ever experienced such an atmosphere. They were too young to have been around in the old days. Theirs was a world of computers, churnalism and clickbait.

Davies, West and Johnson breezed into the newsroom but hardly anyone paid them any attention. Preoccupied journalists stared at their screens, working frenziedly to get their next story out to the masses before another news outlet beat them to it.

There were 20-odd journalists, anxiety evident on their faces as they struggled to cope with the pressure of having to publish a different version every day for each of the three East Midlands' cities as well as constantly updating social media sites.

A photographer slurped coffee, spilling it over a desk and just missing expensive-looking cameras and lenses.

Bill Cooper, a calm, middle-aged news editor with a tanned complexion and alert demeanour, showed them around. They saw journalists rapidly scanning the Internet for a gem of an idea for their next story. Sports journalists were digging up as much background as possible on a footballer who just might be transferred to one of the region's clubs. Digital content editors were dreaming up phrases to convince readers to look at their stories, such as 'chilling footage', 'one to avoid' and 'this can never happen again'.

One wrote: 'When's the storm coming?' Davies smiled as he thought some basketball fans might think they were reading a sports story rather than an extreme weather warning.

Cooper gave them details about Kevin Michaels' career and his achievements, not holding anything back, including the odd failure.

'I don't know how we're going to replace him. He was a legend – so prolific, so knowledgeable. When you were short of a story, he was always the one who could get you a cracking page lead. I'll miss him. He was a fine reporter and a good friend.'

Davies gave a hint of a smile. 'We'll need to speak to everyone who went out for a drink with him last night. Someone will be round later to take statements.'

He then asked Tilly to make a start on checking the archives for any controversial stories that Michaels might have written. He knew she'd have to wade through countless articles featuring Michaels' by-line, from human interest stories to ones holding politicians to account.

In her head she went through some of the most common motives for murder. Sex: unlikely because Michaels appeared to be a committed family man, although it couldn't be entirely ruled out. Money: again unlikely as he didn't appear to be in debt. Revenge: possible because he must have got under the skin of several public figures over the years.

Davies and West spoke to three of Michaels' colleagues who all said he was a great bloke, an asset to the paper and was irreplaceable.

Davies couldn't remember whether it was the French statesman Charles de Gaulle or Winston Churchill who'd come out with the comment 'cemeteries are full of indispensable people'.

It was a different story when they spoke to Simon Powell, a fresh-faced, animated journalist in his mid-twenties.

'Kev wasn't just a workmate – he was one of my best friends. Great guy – he'd do anything for you. Took me under his wing when I came to Nottingham just after I'd qualified as a journalist.

'We all went for a drink yesterday evening but Kev was the first to leave. Made some excuse about getting away early to see Helen and the kids. But he told me he was working on a story and he needed to check something out.

'A while back he did an exclusive about a local charity that tries to stop children being exploited sexually. When he heard some of the tales about those poor little kids . . . well, it really affected him.

Imagined what it would be like if it were his children who'd been groomed or abused.

'He'd heard about a gang who were picking up girls from a care home and plying them with drugs and vodka. Some of your guys were supposed to be aware of what was going on. But Kev thought the police were taking too much time. He wanted to gather some evidence of his own which could get the men arrested more quickly.

'Kev said he was going to see a contact of his, a former drugs squad detective. Works now for some organisation that looks into the main drug dealers and where they get their supplies from.

'I'm worried that someone thought Kev was getting a bit close to the truth. Too close in fact.'

11

PC Catherine Thomas loved her job but knew she'd never earn enough money to buy a property in The Park, one of the most exclusive areas of the city. It was where Rob Woodcock and Felicity Strutt lived although she couldn't imagine how they afforded it.

Whenever she walked from the castle into the private estate she always marvelled at the entrance, with its two majestic-looking gates, tan in colour, one featuring a fleur-de-lis, the other a resplendent peacock.

Today, though, she'd driven from the station and noticed how the sun was struggling to break through the clouds, almost apologising for not shining on this highly sought-after area. Trees fought to hang on to their leaves in the breeze; they seemed to know they had to win the conflict so that The Park maintained its desirability.

Some of the buildings could be described as palatial; the rest were desirable to say the least.

Victorian architecture was the most prominent feature of the area, even though some of the properties had been converted into flats. City planners had grasped for once that this was a conservation area that needed conserving.

The gas street lamps gave the area a Dickensian feel. Catherine half-expected someone dressed as Miss Havisham or Mr Micawber to appear in front of her. It wasn't the sort of place a woman should be on her own at night. Was Felicity Strutt abducted on her way home? Did someone take advantage of the dimly lit street to harm her?

Two people walking up a hill were struggling with their shopping while a hoodie-wearing teenager almost careered into Catherine's car while hurtling downwards. Otherwise, she was struck by how quiet the streets were. It was as if everyone had disappeared for the day, going off to high-powered jobs in the city or commuting long distances for lucrative positions elsewhere.

The burglar alarms above the bay windows of the houses sent out a signal of defiance: try to break in if you dare.

Rob Woodcock showed Catherine into a modern, glitzy apartment. The walls were covered with photographs of his wife.

Felicity looking glamorous.

Felicity looking athletic.

Felicity surrounded by admiring fans as she opened a shop.

A woman who likes herself a lot, Catherine thought.

Woodcock wasted no time in asking whether there was any news about his wife.

'Not yet. But we've got plenty of officers working on the case. We're confident of a breakthrough soon.' The standard non-committal comment.

'But surely you must have found out something by now?'

'We had to be sure that your wife was genuinely missing and hadn't merely gone off without telling you.'

Woodcock sighed in exasperation. 'I told the idiot – sorry, your colleague at the station – there was no way she would have just taken off somewhere without leaving me a note or calling me. She'd let me know exactly where she was going.'

'But you must appreciate that we don't know you or your wife. Until we find out more about her, who she associated with, the places she frequented, we can't rule anything out.'

'Okay, have a good look round. Take anything you want. But please find her – I want her back.'

He led Catherine from the living room with its opulent suite and ostentatious chandelier to the luxuriously appointed bathroom and two bedrooms.

There was a look of astonishment on Catherine's face when they entered the final room. There was no spare bed, only row after row of elegant dresses, designer tops and shoes in every colour imaginable.

Woodcock's voice was close to breaking but he spoke with conviction and pride.

'You may be surprised at what you can see here but Felicity isn't the sort who invites people to stay. She loves her privacy when she's not at work. It's probably because of all the time she spends in the public eye. So we decided the best use for this room would be for Felicity to store her clothes, use it as a dressing room. She's meticulous about her appearance – thinks it wouldn't be good for her image for anyone to see her without make-up or wearing anything from a chain store.'

Catherine paused, wondering if she even dared say what was on her mind.

'I'm sorry to ask this, Mr Woodcock, but how are you able to afford a place like this? I wouldn't have thought a regional TV station pays a big enough salary. Is it rented or have you got a mortgage on it?'

'It's rented. It's all part of Felicity's plan. She only wants to stay in this job for another year. Two at the most. Then she expects to move to London where the best jobs are.

'She lost her parents a couple of years ago. Both killed in a car crash. They were quite wealthy. Felicity was their only child, so she inherited everything.'

Woodcock led Catherine back to the living room. She sat in a luxurious armchair, ignoring the temptation to relax.

'And what about you – do you go along with Felicity's plan?'

'Of course. I should be able to find a job fairly easily in PR in London. That is, if Felicity doesn't need me to be her full-time manager by then.'

His eye focused on the thick, plush carpet before returning to Catherine.

'Some of my friends think I'm stupid to let Felicity have her own way all the time. But it doesn't bother me. I love her. I'd do anything for her. And living in a place like this – not much of a hardship, is it?'

There was the slightest trace of envy as Catherine took in the surroundings.

'Mind if I have another look around?'

Woodcock beckoned for her to go wherever she wanted.

Several minutes later she called Woodcock into Felicity's dressing room, pointing to a glass which had been hidden out of sight on a cupboard shelf. A wedding ring and an engagement ring were just about covered by a clear liquid. Catherine detected a faint smell, one that she recognised straightaway: gin.

'Any idea what this is?' She held up the glass so that Woodcock could see the contents.

'Felicity often puts her rings in gin to clean them. Brings them up really well. But she never goes out without them. Can't understand why she wasn't wearing them when she went to work.'

'I'll take this, if you don't mind. Oh, and one more thing: does Felicity have a laptop?'

'Yes, I'll get it for you.'

Woodcock retrieved it from a shelf underneath an oak coffee table which threatened to take over the whole room. Catherine wasn't surprised to see that the laptop was the latest model, without a mark on it, and stored in a leather case that reeked of newness and a high price.

'Do you ever use it?'

There was a note of resignation in Woodcock's voice. 'No, I've got my own. Never need to borrow Felicity's. Mind you, she doesn't use it a lot, apart from accessing a few news websites and putting the odd thing on Facebook, Twitter, Instagram. Unlike some people she's not addicted to social media.'

'So you won't be surprised at anything we find on her laptop?'

'Not at all. We don't have any secrets.'

Catherine's facial expression didn't change.

'What about trolls – do many people make unpleasant comments about her?'

'Occasionally. It's usually people who are jealous of her success. They think she got her job just because she's attractive. They don't understand how much hard work she's had to put in to get where she is.'

'And that's her only computer?'

'That's right. She does use one at the office. But she hot-desks. Other people use the same PC.'

'What about fan mail – does she get much?' asked Catherine.

Woodcock beamed with pride. 'You wouldn't believe in this day and age how many people still post letters to her. She gets far more than anyone else at the station. And of course emails. She doesn't give her work email address out but you'd be surprised how many people manage to guess what it is. I help Felicity to answer a lot of the letters and emails. They ask for signed photos, locks of her hair, all sorts. She even gets requests for her underwear.'

'How does it make you feel, imagining what some of those guys are up to?'

Woodcock smiled, a sense of satisfaction lighting up his eyes.

'I don't think about it. I just tell myself that at the end of the day I'm the one she goes to bed with.'

12

Alexandra Wright finished her examination and took off her disposable gloves, goggles, face mask and white lab coat. The forensic pathologist's make-up was perfect even though she'd been in the lab for the past couple of hours. Her cheeks glowed without appearing too red, her eyes had the right amount of mascara to give her a sensual look and her lipstick was pale yet classy.

Her mouth was never still as she chewed gum with the vigour of a diner chomping on an underdone steak. She completed her notes, moved into the adjoining office and picked up the phone.

'Miles, you gorgeous thing, how are you?'

'Hi Alex. To what do I owe the pleasure? Don't tell me – you just want a decent conversation. All those bodies you've got down there – not much company because they don't answer back.'

'I admit it can get a bit lonely down here and you always brighten my day. I can't think of anything better than hearing your sexy voice on the other end of a telephone – unless it's having you next to me in the flesh.'

Davies laughed. 'Can't you think of anything better to say than that? I've lost count of the number of times you've trotted that one out.'

She sighed. 'Doesn't take much to make me happy. And I've told you before: you and I could be brilliant together – but for some indescribable reason you won't take me up on it.'

Davies got on really well with Alex Wright but that was as far as it went. He admired her on a professional level but there was no physical attraction.

His main regret was the night they'd both been out to celebrate the retirement of a well-respected but boring colleague. After a few too many drinks they'd slipped off early, got a taxi and Davies foolishly accepted an invitation for a nightcap at Alex's house.

They'd ended up in bed, much to Alex's delight but Davies' shame because he'd taken advantage of her while he wasn't fully in control of himself. It took him a long time to get over his guilt and Alex even longer before she admitted to herself that their tryst would be an unforgettable one-off.

'Anyway,' she continued, 'I've got something you'll be interested in. Kevin Michaels. If you hadn't told me what had happened to him, I would have assumed he was involved in a hit-and-run. Forty-odd fractures, blunt-force injuries to his head, face and chest. Brain damage too. Looks as though someone jumped on his face and chest repeatedly. This was a severe assault. I've never seen anything like it.'

A full ten seconds passed before Davies could return to efficient police officer mode.

'So, what actually killed him?'

'Well, his head was smashed against something blunt which probably finished him off. As well as head trauma he had acute internal haemorrhage and organ failure, so take your pick. It must have been a blessed relief for him. Who on earth could be so heartless?'

Davies thought about all the criminals he'd come across who would have no hesitation in carrying out such a brutal, inhumane assault.

'Thanks, Alex. Anything else?'

'It's not for me to tell you your job but I reckon you're looking for a man whose hands are in a bad way. You don't give someone a beating like that and not suffer yourself. And I should think a vehicle was used to transport the body – there'll be blood all over it.'

'What about the fountain pen?'

'Might have caused him a slight problem if he hadn't been so savagely attacked. By then the damage had been done.'

Davies' mind was in a whirl: what had Kevin Michaels done to deserve such a gory death? What was the killer's motive: did he want something kept secret? And why stick a fountain pen in Michaels when he was virtually dead anyway?

13

'Ayup, Ken.' The voice of a teenager in a hooded top and faded, ripped jeans. It was bravado usually associated with someone several years older.

'Morning, young man. Hope you're behaving yourself.'

'Course I am. Why shouldn't I?'

'Well, I've been hearing that you've been a bad lad – nicking car hub caps, damaging fences, that sort of thing. What do they call it now? Anti-social behaviour. You'll get yourself into trouble before too long.'

'Nah, nobody will catch me.'

Thompson went up to him, put his hand on the youngster's shoulder and squeezed.

'Look here, son. It's time you started listening to what your mum tells you. Mum's always right – don't you ever forget that. You won't make her proud if you end up in court. Get yourself sorted out. For a start, go to school and learn as much as you can. Oh, I know, school's boring. But do you want to spend your whole life in an area like this?'

The warmth in his voice put the youngster at ease. Thompson continued: 'If you could do any job, what would it be?'

'Footballer. Or pop star. So I can earn loads of money. And get plenty of girls!'

'Well, you won't succeed if you don't get the best education you can. Anything else?'

The teenager went quiet, then jumped up as if a few hundred volts had been pumped into his body.

'Cars. I want to drive around all day in flash cars.'

'I can't promise you a job doing that. But I tell you what: you do your best at school and I'll pull a few strings, see what I can do. Is that a deal?'

His eyes blazed with enthusiasm. 'Okay, Ken, yeah.'

Thompson gave him a playful kick up the backside and the teenager trotted off, his head held high.

The television building was modern and an unremarkable piece of architecture. Yet people who'd never been inside found it exciting, even glamorous. Television was the glittering, magical enigma that could get them their much sought-after 15 minutes of fame and help them to become a celebrity no matter how minuscule their talent.

West and Davies, trying hard to supress his displeasure at having to investigate a missing person case while his team were in the early stages of a murder inquiry, were shown up to the first floor. The walls were adorned with slogans such as 'audiences are at the heart of everything we do', 'we take pride in delivering quality and value for money' and 'great things happen when we work together'.

Journalists, production staff and presenters packed the L-shaped office, half of them on telephones, the rest checking the Internet and social media for their next programme idea.

A trim, elegant, middle-aged woman ushered the two detectives into a relatively small, orderly office. Several awards were hanging on the walls, most of them handed out in the past couple of years. Proof of how successful the station had become.

Alongside them were pictures of rugby players involved in major triumphs: Jonny Wilkinson kicking the drop goal which won England the World Cup in 2003; London Wasps who lifted the Heineken Cup in 2007; the Leicester Tigers' line-up which landed both the league and play-offs for the second successive season in 2010.

The aroma of a strong, unsophisticated aftershave hung in the air, stopping the two policemen momentarily as the smell invaded their nostrils.

'Hello, gentlemen. Good to meet you. Sorry it's in these circumstances.'

Davies could hardly be described as short but Chris Watson towered over him. A former rugby second-row forward who'd represented his country, Watson pursued his interest in the media during the final days of his professional career. His good name on the sports field enabled him to get a job in broadcasting; his managerial skills meant his promotion to a top position was far faster than he'd ever been on the turf at Twickenham.

Now, in open-necked shirt, jacket and jeans, Watson still looked like a sportsman rather than an executive.

'Felicity is probably the most liked person on the station. We just can't understand what's happened to her.' He gulped.

'Mr Watson, she is, at this stage, only missing. Have you *any* idea where she might be?'

'No. She's not one for going off without telling anyone where she is. If she's out filming and the location changes or there's a health and safety risk, she's onto the office straightaway.'

Without prompting, Watson praised the station's star asset: 'She's a remarkable, warm young woman. She lights up a room whenever she walks in. I can guarantee that everyone you talk to will tell you the same thing.

'She was nominated for an award last year for best on-screen personality. They didn't give it to her – it went to someone who'd been doing the job for much longer. Sometimes experience is rewarded more than talent. I'm sure she's going to win it this year.'

He anticipated Davies's next question.

'I can't think of anyone who might want to hurt her. I'm sure that none of the staff have had an argument with her. Not even a cross word. Some of her weather forecasts might have been a bit inaccurate – but she's never got a hurricane wrong.'

Fawning praise. Davies wanted to know whether Felicity was as perfect as Watson made out: 'Did she have any ambitions – did she think she could do a better job than some of the more experienced staff? Or did she think she wasn't given enough opportunities to use her talents?'

Watson shifted uncomfortably despite having the best and most expensive seat in the building.

'She wasn't what you'd call fiercely ambitious – she just wanted to do the best job she possibly could. I reckon she could have a great future on an entertainment show, but she says she can't stand how shallow and trivial that side of television has become.

'Maybe deep down she wants to do something with a bit more gravitas, something that could make a difference. But as far as I know, she's perfectly happy presenting the weather for the time being.'

He looked down at the thick, luxurious, heavily patterned carpet before continuing.

'There is a possible explanation: she might be a victim of one of the people we call Sunday psychos.'

Quizzical looks from both detectives.

'They're the people who tune in on Sunday evenings and then send messages on social media to our female presenters. Sexist messages come in during the week as well but the women get bombarded with them on Sundays. Obviously some people have nothing else to do at the weekend.'

Davies assured Watson that someone would check Felicity's online profiles.

'Now, will you excuse me? The lunchtime bulletin will be on air shortly. You can watch from the gallery if you like, see how it all comes together.'

The two detectives nodded their agreement. Watson took them down the stairs past the studio into the gallery where staff were quietly preparing for transmission.

One wall of the air-conditioned, windowless room was filled with 50 monitors showing everything from different camera angles of the studio to the teleprompter which allowed the presenter to follow the words rather than reading a script.

Computer screens, mixing desks and microphones were dotted around yet despite the huge amount of equipment there was enough space for people to work without feeling hemmed in.

'The monitors with "TX" underneath them in red are the ones you need to watch when we go live,' Watson whispered to his guests. 'The director's in charge here – you keep the noise down so that everyone can hear her when she decides what we're going to next, either a report that's been pre-recorded or to an outside broadcast.'

The director stared in Watson's direction, eager to let him know she wouldn't tolerate any noise, no matter who it was from.

'Okay, everyone: script check, please.' The heavy Dublin accent was overflowing with authority; she could induce apprehension in anyone who didn't know her.

She quickly ran through the running order, allowing enough time for the presenter to mark on her back-up script which of the three cameras she should be looking at when they went on air for real.

'Right, let's rehearse sequence two, the first OB. Cue Madeleine.'

The presenter began to read a story about a man allegedly killing his lover on Christmas Eve before dumping her body in the River Trent. Madeleine introduced the reporter, sixty-year-old Gordon Bailey, a man with a bulbous, scarlet nose and full, ruddy cheeks who was standing outside the city's Crown Court.

Bailey, appearing nervous and uncomfortable in front of the camera, stuttered and stumbled his way through the morning's evidence. When asked a question about the prosecution's opening statement he hesitated before answering, as if startled by what he'd heard in his earpiece.

When the practice run was over, the PA – responsible for ensuring everything ran to its allotted time – pressed a switch: 'Gordon, love, you were forty-five seconds over. Can you cut it down a bit?'

Bailey nodded, resignation etched on his face.

Davies and West looked at each other, not knowing what to expect once the programme went on air. But after the opening titles and Bailey was introduced, the reporter came alive. He was knowledgeable and delivered the entire piece without stumbling once or looking at his notes.

At the end of the bulletin, the director thanked everyone for their endeavours and the staff headed off for lunch.

'Impressed?' asked Watson.

'Very,' returned Davies.

'A couple of questions,' said West. 'The presenter can see the words that she reads. What do you call that – is it the autocue?'

Watson nodded.

'It looked as though the reporter outside the Crown Court wasn't reading. Is that correct? Did he have to memorise the words he was going to say?'

'You're right,' said Watson. 'It's far too expensive to have a portable autocue on location. It's only the big national programmes which have that luxury. So yes, reporters have to remember what they're going to say when they go live. Often they don't get long to do it. It's quite an art to make it sound conversational as well as authoritative.'

West's eyes showed amazement as he carried on with what was almost turning into an interrogation: 'During the rehearsal the reporter appeared to be taken unawares by the question from the presenter. Is there any way to stop that happening?'

Watson smiled, a smug look engulfing his face. 'That's what a lot of people want to know. It might be different working for a national TV channel where everything is more frantic and they just don't have time for a rehearsal. But here in the regions a reporter should never be flummoxed by what the presenter says. That's because the reporter always writes the questions.'

14

For two hours after lunch Davies and West were subjected to gushing statements from several of Felicity's colleagues about what a wonderful person the weather presenter was.

As the pair of them walked back down the stairs, Davies dropped his voice although no one was near them.

'What do you make of Watson? Is he telling the truth?'

'Definitely not. He thinks the sun shines out of Felicity's backside. Perhaps he sees her as a way of getting more gongs to stick on the wall.'

'Did you get a close look at him?' asked Davies. 'Didn't maintain eye contact for long. And he was fidgeting quite a bit too. He's hiding something. I just wish someone would tell us about the *real* Felicity Strutt.'

They were heading for the exit when Gordon Bailey sidled up to them. 'There's a coffee shop about 200 yards up the road. Can you meet me there in ten minutes?'

The reporter got there first, picked up his order and sat down. His hand shook as he picked up his cup. Alcohol was his downfall; it had led to the end of virtually every job he'd talked himself into.

Long-serving staff at the television station advised the management not to take him on because of his reputation – his aggression and vitriol when he'd had a few drinks were known throughout the journalism industry. But Chris Watson's predecessor decided that Bailey's newsgathering skills and extensive list of contacts made him invaluable when he was sober. The seasoned hack was so grateful he vowed to stay off the drink and he was true to his word – in the short term.

Davies sat down while West went to the counter.

'We saw you on the lunchtime news. Very professional job. What's happening with the court case?'

'Adjourned for the day. Defence starts tomorrow morning.'

West brought coffee and a selection of cakes.

Davies ignored his drink for the time being. 'Is there something you want to tell us?'

Bailey's arm remained still just long enough for him to sip his coffee before returning his cup to the table.

'Don't believe everything they tell you about Felicity Strutt.'

'You're not trying to tell me that butter *would* melt in her mouth?'

'They're a good bunch over there. Really nice atmosphere. It's one of the best places I've ever worked. But they're not telling you everything about that woman.'

Davies notice the venom in Bailey's voice when he said *that woman*.

'Why's that?'

'I dunno. They all stick together. I don't suppose you'd like it if someone slagged off one of your friends. They won't have anything bad said about any of their colleagues. Not in public, anyway. I just want the truth to come out. There are two Felicity Strutts – one the public sees and the real one off-screen.'

'So who's the real Felicity?'

'She's as hard as nails. Ruthless. She wants to be on national TV – present a documentary or become an investigative journalist. There aren't any openings here at the moment – but that won't stop her. She'll claw her way to the top. No one will stand in her way. Mark my words, when it happens people will start to talk differently about her.'

Davies took a sip of his latte, mulling over Bailey's opinion of Felicity.

'That's not what Chris Watson told us.'

'Well, he's got – what shall we say? – an ulterior motive.'

'Meaning?'

'Let's just say he's been behaving in an unusual way. Doesn't usually socialise with the staff. But he's taken Felicity out for a meal more than once.'

West jumped in: 'Who would want to get rid of her then – one of the regular presenters?'

'No. They're well established. They're good. Well paid. They're not too old, so the management aren't looking to get rid of them. Especially as the viewing figures keep going up.'

'How about one of the reporters?'

'Doubtful. Felicity's done a few weather-related stories but nothing else. I shouldn't think any of the reporters feel threatened by her.'

Davies noticed Bailey start to tremble again. His fists tightened and he stiffened, trying not to show how uncomfortable he'd become. He would have preferred something stronger than coffee.

'I'll bet my house that she doesn't want to do just the weather. She's after so much more. But let me tell you this: there's an old saying in journalism that news is what someone *doesn't* want reported. It wouldn't surprise me to hear she's uncovered a scandal that would cause ructions if it got out. I reckon that's why she's disappeared.'

15

Davies welcomed his team back to the incident room for the late-afternoon briefing. 'Good to see you all again. Doesn't seem like five minutes since we were here this morning.

'Had a good day, Mark? Plenty to get your teeth into?'

Mark Roberts smiled as he passed around notes for everyone.

'I've gone through Kevin Michaels' phone records and nothing seems to jump out at me. The only repeat calls are to his office and home.

'House-to-house have been talking to neighbours but nothing much from them. Some thought Michaels was a bit stuck up and wouldn't speak to them. Others thought he was a nice enough bloke despite the job he did. A couple even said he kept himself to himself. Imagine that, an introverted newspaper reporter. Highly unlikely. So we've categorised the people who made those comments as not wanting to get involved. Don't you just love the public?'

Davies gave him a stern look but Roberts carried on regardless and projected an image onto the wall.

'The most useful thing we've got is CCTV footage. This is Michaels coming out of the Smithfield. Just after 9pm. Sets off towards the bus station. But then we lose him. We're trying to find out where he went after leaving the pub before his body was found six miles away a few hours later.'

Davies picked up a report he'd been handed just before the meeting.

'Here are the DNA results. The killer's left traces all over his victim and the crime scene – but there's no match on the database.

'As for the fountain pen that was found stuck in his chest, it was black with a medium nib and blue ink, the sort you can buy from any stationer's for a few pounds. But that didn't kill him – he took a severe beating and we think the pen was symbolic. We've yet to decipher what it means.'

A voice came from the middle of the room.

'I've seen Michaels in court a few times. Do you think one of the criminals he reported on wanted revenge?'

'Possibly,' said Davies. 'I want someone to check if any major criminals have been released from prison in the past few months. See if Michaels had any links to them. In the meantime Tilly's going to be looking through Michaels' reports. He was a prolific writer, so it may take time before she finds anything that looks odd.

'So who is the murderer? Is he playing a game with us? What's he trying to tell us?

'Has he killed before? It's possible – so we need to check any unsolved murders to see if there's any comparison.'

As Davies turned to Felicity Strutt's disappearance, Detective Superintendent Holland made his way into the room.

'What's her background?' asked Davies.

Allen picked up a file and read from the top page. 'Nothing that sticks out. Studied geography at university. First-class degree. Joined the uni drama group as soon as she got there but by year three she'd given it up, presumably to concentrate on her studies. So you couldn't really call her a drama queen.'

The usual derision and groans whenever Allen uttered one of his quips.

'She also got involved in the students' radio station. Presented her own show for a while. Until they took her off the air. I've spoken to the guy who was head of the station at the time. Reckoned she was too aloof – wasn't on the same wavelength as the rest of the students. Always talking about herself. He said she'd perfected the art of narrowcasting, not broadcasting.'

Davies' fingers met in front of his lips as he considered what he'd just heard.

'Anything more recent?'

'Got a job with the TV station not long after graduating. She's thought of as a rising star. Presents the weather with a smile. Makes even the shittiest day sound not as bad as it really is. They reckon she could be heading for London before too long. Nice face, looks great on camera. She's regarded as a serious scientist rather than a brolly dolly. Seems as though she's got everything. But from some of the comments on social media, she's recognised for her high-pressure front rather than her intimacy with isobars.'

Davies' face remained passive. 'Private life?'

'Met Robert Woodcock, account executive for a PR company, not long after she moved to the area. Shacked up together shortly afterwards and a few months later they got married. Seem a perfectly normal couple.'

'Thanks for that.'

A uniformed officer chimed up: 'Sir, you asked us to go house to house and see what we could come up with. Well, there's a guy who reckons he heard the Woodcocks arguing like crazy the night before she disappeared. Lives next door. Says they were shouting at the tops of their voices. They were making such a racket it woke up his young child. In the end he banged on their door and threatened to call the police.

'The noise subsided a bit, but the neighbour says Felicity was still having a go at her husband. He went quiet for a while, but then the neighbour heard him say, "Do that and you're a dead woman".'

'Only one thing for it, then,' Holland interjected. 'Bring him in. Let's see him wriggle out of that.'

Davies' expression showed the officer he was grateful. Far be it from Holland to thank anyone for a job well done.

'We're holding a press conference in the morning,' the Detective Superintendent said. 'I'm sure there won't be a shortage of people who can tell us what might have happened to Felicity – but my money's on the husband.'

16

Davies jumped in his car and drove without breaking the speed limit along the A52 to Derby. He had just enough time to make the start of the Derby Storm game against one of their intense rivals, Sheffield Sharks.

He arrived just as the announcer bellowed: 'Please welcome your very own home-town Derby Storrrrrrm!' The thunderous roar and the electric atmosphere reaffirmed why Davies preferred basketball to any other sport.

But within minutes he was fidgeting in his seat. The Storm were struggling and there was more tension on his face than when he was undergoing a difficult cross-examination in a Crown Court case.

Despite that, he felt at home when he was watching basketball. From the first time he picked up a ball at school, he was hooked. He loved the pace, the excitement, the competitiveness. At one time the Sharks were a team that Derby looked up to; they were successful on a regular basis and boasted a solid fan base. Now the Storm were a good match for them.

He felt invigorated when the Storm were winning – but he and hundreds of supporters became grumpy when they weren't playing well. He wished he could adopt the attitude shown by a former Storm coach who advised his players never to get too excited after a victory or too despondent after a loss. Still, that coach wasn't one who practised what he preached, so why should Davies keep his emotions in check?

Apart from that, Davies had seen the old Storm collapse. The city had been without a professional basketball club for several years before a businessman with an eye for an opportunity decided to resurrect the team.

He provided the money for a purpose-built arena with two practice courts. Parts of it were hired out for everything from corporate events to dog shows. The Storm were one of the few clubs to have their own venue so that they weren't dependent solely on income generated by the sport.

The new owner also found the cash to bring in a highly-rated, young American coach who put together a team that looked capable of winning a trophy. So Davies was determined to see as much of the Storm's season as possible; watching the game against Sheffield would give him a bit of a break before he turned his mind back to the Kevin Michaels case.

The anticipation he'd experienced when he arrived at the Storm Arena evaporated by half time as Derby were trailing by 20 points to the Sharks. It looked like the Storm would suffer a humiliating home defeat. Davies thought momentarily about buying a new pair of basketball boots and trying out for the team. Surely he couldn't be any worse than some of those on the court? But he realised he had neither the time nor the stamina.

Yet Derby gradually hauled themselves back into the game, chipping away at Sheffield's lead and bringing the partisan crowd to life.

Leading by one point inside the last twenty seconds, the Sharks mounted one last offence in a bid to put the game out of Derby's reach. Davies and everyone around him leapt to their feet as Sheffield's point guard threw up a shot which bounced off the rim and was gobbled up by Yandel Eliot.

He found Rick Parker who glanced at the clock and realised there was still time to win the game.

He saw Eliot tearing down the floor with a couple of Sheffield players struggling to get back on defence. Parker waited, timed his pass to perfection and bounced it to Eliot who caught it cleanly.

With no one around him he took off thirteen feet from the basket and made sure he was gripping the ball firmly in his right hand. The crowd held their breath, expecting Eliot to hammer the ball, tomahawk-fashion, through the hoop. But it hit the back of the rim and bounced on a high trajectory towards the rafters. It had only just started its downward flight when the buzzer sounded the end of the game.

Storm fans were despondent. 'What an idiot. Coach should have a word with him. You don't get any more points for a dunk. Ought to have made sure instead of showboating,' complained one supporter.

His friend agreed. 'Eliot had a pretty good game. Just spoilt it with that attempt at a dunk. That's why he's playing in Derby and not the NBA.'

As Davies left the Arena he heard another fan remark: 'Shame about the end. If we'd beaten the Sharks it would have got a good slot on the TV news. But the defeat means they'll probably stick it in its usual place, just before the weather.'

Davies suddenly thought about Felicity Strutt. Why hadn't she gone for a drink with her colleagues? Who did she meet after work? Was there more to her disappearance than met the eye? And would they find her dead just like Kevin Michaels?

Davies was getting himself a drink at the bar and listening to fans still re-living highlights of the game when he heard a familiar voice.

'Hello, sir, didn't expect to see you here.'

Tilly Johnson was casually dressed in a white blouse and jeans. Her hair, tied back when she was working, hung loosely over her shoulders. She was wearing hardly any make-up and looked even more attractive than Davies remembered.

'Didn't expect to see you, either. You a basketball fan, then?'

'Absolutely. Some friends got me into the sport a few years ago. The standard wasn't very high in Norfolk and I really missed it. So I thought I'd give the Storm a go.'

'Sorry, very remiss of me. Can I get you a drink?'

'Just an orange juice. I'm driving.' She laughed. 'Don't want to get breathalysed on the way home.'

They adjourned to a corner table as the bar started to fill up.

'Are you a regular here as well, sir? Can't say I've noticed you at a ball game before.'

'I get here whenever I can. And there's no need to call me sir when we're off duty. Miles will do.'

Her eyes beamed as she smiled. 'So, are you new to basketball?'

'Not at all. I was introduced to the sport at school. I was rubbish at football and rugby but with basketball I could make a contribution. Played for a local league team as well – but I wasn't good enough to take it any further.

'Still get a kick out of watching. And I called my son Jordan, after the world's finest basketball player.'

'Would you like him to play professionally? Maybe make it big in the NBA?'

'It'll be up to him. I won't push him into doing anything he doesn't want to do. My father wanted me to emulate him and become a musician – but I never took to playing an instrument.'

His eyes slumped as he recalled the dance bands and jazz groups that his father had joined. He'd also played on studio sessions and accompanied artists whose albums had become best sellers.

When Miles was born his parents named him after the influential trumpeter Miles Davis. Young Miles went to piano lessons at an early age but he didn't show a natural talent for music. At school he learned a few notes on the recorder but it was obvious he wasn't going to follow in his father's footsteps.

His parents were fiercely proud of him when he announced he was joining the police.

'Jordan's only seven,' Miles told Tilly. 'He can choose whatever career he wants. But if he decides to play basketball there are far more opportunities now than when I was a lad. I know a couple of young guys who've gone to the States. Playing in college. Another graduated and he's joined a club in Germany. If my son wants to do that, I'll support him all the way. If not, I'll be behind him whatever he decides to do.'

'You sound like a good dad who really loves his son.'

'Aren't all fathers like that?'

17

Ken Thompson stretched, his ample frame taking up most of his extra-large bed. He looked up to see his reflection in the huge mirror he'd installed on the ceiling and chuckled as he remembered nights of uninhibited lust with women he'd taken back to his house. He wasn't keen on letting many people know where he lived but there were some evenings when a pretty woman caught his eye and he just couldn't resist temptation.

He didn't need an alarm clock; he liked to get plenty of business out of the way before many other people had emerged from under their duvet.

He looked around the room with its zebra-print bedding, splashes of red in the curtains and abstract paintings. He liked what he saw. He'd chosen everything in the bedroom himself – he'd left the rest of the house to a professional. Thompson had impressed on the effeminate, flamboyant interior designer that he wanted tasteful, not tacky – and the man would never work again if he messed up.

Thompson walked down the stairs, past his sumptuous cinema room kitted out with the latest technological advances, through the living room with its crystal-encrusted sofa and into the kitchen.

He ignored the ridiculously expensive coffee machine which he hardly ever used and switched on the kettle. Tea: best drink of all at this time of day.

He threw a pile of cornflakes into a bowl and dropped two slices of white bread into the toaster. As he wolfed down the cereal he looked out of the window; everything was quiet, nothing moved apart from the odd pigeon flittering from tree to tree – just as he liked it.

The house was set back from the road. It had its own drive with trees on either side but little that required regular maintenance from a gardener. It was private enough to keep out anyone who didn't have business with Thompson. But the property wasn't so ostentatious as to attract inquisitive sightseers who wanted to pry into how rich people lived.

He shouldn't really have done anything to the house; he refused to buy a property in case the police came snooping and tried to seize it as an asset, so he rented. His landlord was suddenly forced to disappear abroad and had no qualms about Thompson doing it up to his own specifications. Money paid into an offshore bank account every month kept the owner happy.

The toast popped up and a woman's voice boomed across the kitchen.

'Ooh, I'm sorry, Mr Thompson. You startled me. I didn't fink you wuz here.'

'That's all right, Monica. Had a quiet night in last night. Left the car in the garage. And how many times have I told you to call me Ken?'

'You don't mind if I get on with the cleaning, do you?'

'Course not. Unless you want a brew first.'

'I'll 'ave one later, if that's all right. Need to crack on.'

The kettle boiled and Thompson made tea.

'Don't work too hard. And take a break whenever you need one. By the way, how's the family?'

'Oh, they're grand. David's just got himself a job in a sports shop. 'E absolutely loves it. The pay ain't very good. But I suppose it's a start.'

'Pleased to hear it. Let me know if I can help out in any way.'

'Thanks, Ken. You're all 'eart.'

Thompson slugged down his drink, put the cup in the dishwasher and moved towards the door.

'I've got to go out now, Monica. I may be a while, so don't hang around here all day. And make sure you cook your David something nice for his tea.'

18

Detectives were laughing and joking as they met in the incident room for the morning update.

It was like any other office in the building, full of desks chosen for their functionality rather than aesthetic qualities, banks of computers everywhere, files and paperwork piled up on any available surface. So much for the paperless era.

Paul Allen caught everyone's attention with an announcement: 'We've got another murder. A guy killed with a piece of sandpaper. Seems the killer went too far – he was only trying to rough him up a bit!'

Groans could be heard around the room as Davies gave him a stern look. 'Come on, now, let's get cracking. Mark, what's the latest on Kevin Michaels?'

Roberts jumped to his feet, eager to share what he'd discovered about the newspaper man.

'Early in his career he was one of twenty-eight people who were sacked by the Nottingham Post. They'd gone on strike – it was a dispute by journalists in the provinces that affected newspapers all over the country.

'Strange because the journalists in Nottingham were relatively happy with what they were being paid. I bet you wouldn't find that now. Anyway, back in 1978 they downed their notebooks and pencils. Reckoned they were standing solid with low-paid reporters in the north and were fighting for better conditions.

'It rebounded on the Nottingham lads – the Post was the only paper not to take the strikers back when the industrial action ended. Said they'd been disloyal.

'At the time Michaels was a union activist. There were various allegations from both the journalists and the management – assaults, threats and the like – but nothing ever went to court.

'Something must have happened – a reconciliation or the newspaper changed hands – because a few years later Michaels was working for the Post again.'

Roberts looked up from his papers. 'Boss, don't know how significant that was, but there's nothing else that arouses even the slightest suspicion about Kevin Michaels. Seems to have turned into a family man who quietly got on with his job.'

Davies moved on to the Felicity Strutt case. 'Any sightings of her?'

Now it was West's turn to get to his feet. He looked alert, far more than he'd done twenty-four hours previously.

'In a word, boss, no. The guys have gone through the CCTV and there's no doubt she left the office just after seven o'clock. We tracked her up part of Mansfield Road – but there's nothing on the camera at the junction of Oxclose Lane. There's a hotel in that area, so uniform are seeing if she checked in there.'

'Any news on her car? Somebody must have clocked it.'

'No, boss, seems to have disappeared. Just like her.'

He addressed the whole team: 'Okay. Let's keep at it. We still need CCTV of the area where Kevin Michaels was found. Let's make that a priority. Check with all the taxi companies to see if anyone picked him up after he left the Smithfield. Did he catch a bus? He wasn't far from the bus station, so he could have been waylaid on the way home.

'And why would someone be interested in Felicity? She's an attractive woman, there's no doubt about that. But has she gone away of her own accord or has something sinister happened? Let's widen the search and check the airport to see if she booked a ticket anywhere.

'Is there anything to link Michaels' murder and Felicity Strutt's disappearance?

'I also want as much background as possible on Rob Woodcock. Felicity Strutt was a real extrovert, so maybe he was jealous of some of the people she came in contact with.

'And see if there are any clues to this mystery man she was supposed to be meeting after work. First of all we need to establish whether she was having an affair. Then we can look at other theories. We can't rule out the possibility that someone wanted to do her harm.

But she might have wanted to start a new life and not tell her husband about it.'

19

The beaming face of chief press officer Adam Walton greeted Davies. Walton, a former television reporter, was a popular figure in the force: he knew how to get media coverage and, when necessary, he was adept at keeping inquisitive journalists away from senior officers.

Wearing a smart, off-the-peg suit, blue shirt and sober tie, with his hair kept short and beard well-trimmed, he was always ready to appear in front of the cameras if anyone needed him unexpectedly to make an official statement. He endeavoured to give the press exactly what they were looking for – but made sure he didn't alienate his bosses by giving too much away.

'The press conference is set up. It should be fairly straightforward.'

Davies made sure no one was in earshot. 'Do me a favour, will you? Detective Superintendent Holland's running the show. Can you get one of your reporter mates to give him a hard time?'

'Shouldn't be a problem. Leave it to me.'

Shortly afterwards Holland joined Davies and Walton, the three of them walking into a room that had been converted to host the press conference. Boards featuring the force's logo provided a backdrop behind three chairs and a small table.

'Couldn't you have found a bigger room than this?' Holland whispered to Walton. 'This could be big news. It may get national coverage.'

'We're not expecting many. It's plenty big enough. The local reporter for the Press Association is here and if any of the network TV or radio stations want it, they'll rely on their regional offices to provide them with coverage.'

A handful of journalists, three camera crews and a couple of photographers were waiting for Detective Superintendent Holland to come up with anything useful which would fill their columns and news bulletins.

He outlined the investigation into Kevin Michaels' death and asked for anyone who had information, no matter how trivial the details might seem, to get in touch with the police.

He then concentrated on Felicity Strutt's disappearance, giving it more prominence than he did the murder. He adopted a concerned yet earnest tone: 'What we'd really like to find out is who Felicity arranged to meet on the evening she disappeared. It could have been a business associate, the chief executive of a major company or a representative of a charity. I understand she performed a lot of charity work.'

He looked straight into the nearest camera lens: 'Now, if you're that person who was supposed to be meeting up with Felicity, please come forward so that we can eliminate you from our inquiries.'

He again stressed with as much sincerity as he could muster that the mystery man or woman should perform his or her public duty. Then he invited questions.

Gordon Bailey jumped in: 'We were sorry to hear about Kevin Michaels' murder. It's always tough when we have to report on one of our own suffering such a terrible death.

'But what everyone in this room and the general public want to know is: what's happened to Felicity? And what progress have you made trying to find her?'

His voice became louder and belligerent. 'So far you haven't told us anything we don't know already. You've appealed for help – why have the public always got to do your job for you? Are you so incompetent that you can't track her down on your own?'

Holland spluttered. He hesitated a moment too long before answering.

'My team under DI Davies is working extremely hard on this case. We're following up several lines of inquiry and we're hoping to make a breakthrough soon.'

'Are you linking her disappearance with Kevin Michaels' murder? We're talking here about a high-profile TV presenter who's vanished into thin air. Has she been murdered? Has a stalker kidnapped her? Go on, admit it, you haven't got a clue where she is, have you?'

Holland fingered his shirt collar, his cheeks turning scarlet by the second. He muttered something about hoping for new leads and declared the press conference over before stomping out of the room.

'Bloody hell, who rattled his cage?' Holland eyed Walton with suspicion.

'Don't know what that was all about,' said the press officer. 'I've discussed with him how journalists don't ask the right questions at press conferences – but I didn't think he'd got an attitude problem . . .'

'Who was that?'

'Gordon Bailey, TV reporter. Good operator but likes a drink. Several, to be exact.'

'Miles, check out Bailey's background. I want to know everything about him.'

'Okay, but he's probably worried because there's no news about Felicity. They're work colleagues. Probably close. Don't hold his behaviour against him.'

'I couldn't care less what's bothering him. No one talks to me like that. Now, get me every last detail about him – and quick.'

20

Ken Thompson was a hero in part of the city. But in other areas the name spelt fear; it meant terror; it signified danger for anyone who crossed him.

Thompson could afford to look after those around him because he was probably the biggest crime boss in Nottingham, if not the East Midlands. He made his money through people trafficking, a protection racket and a massive drugs operation. Other drug dealers either suffered intimidation and left the county or disappeared before Thompson showed them why his reputation was so fearsome.

He had dozens of suppliers who distributed cannabis, cocaine and heroin across four counties. But he made sure the drugs could never be traced back to him.

Managers of clubs and bars across the region made regular payments to Thompson to ensure their operation ran smoothly. There was no trouble at all in those licensed premises; the police never had any reason to visit them either by appointment or unannounced.

'Damien, get your coat on. We're going out.'

Damien Henderson was one of the people whose loyalty to Thompson had never been called into question. If it wasn't for Thompson, Damien would more than likely be in prison.

The youngest of a family of six who between them had four different fathers, Damien never experienced the love he needed from his alcohol-dependent mother while his father did a rapid disappearing act – much like his siblings' fathers.

Damien was considered a hopeless case at school, had little chance of persuading an employer to give him even the most menial job and drifted aimlessly through life for the best part of ten years. He came to the notice of the police when he stole from shops, daubed graffiti on walls and damaged the odd bit of property – it was his way of giving his humdrum life a tiny bit of excitement.

When Thompson showed an interest in Damien and got him to run a few errands for which he was paid handsomely, the young man finally had a purpose, a reason to get up in the morning. He formed a bond with Thompson and looked on him as a father figure.

Since meeting Thompson, Damien had never felt so good – not even as a child on Christmas Day. The festive period had never been a brilliant time when he was younger; his five brothers and sisters always seemed to get more presents than he did and whenever he was given something he'd set his heart on, one of his brothers usually broke it before Boxing Day was over.

After severing all ties with his family, he scraped together as much money as he could lay his hands on to pursue his one real passion:

cars. He cleaned toilets, served in a couple of pubs and worked as a casual labourer doing back-breaking work just to save up for driving lessons. He got himself an understanding instructor who wasn't concerned about Damien's inability to make regular bookings.

Sometimes he went for weeks without a lesson when work was hard to come by. But his dedication paid off and he passed his test first time.

Now he had his reward: driving Ken Thompson around in a gleaming, new, luxurious car. Tinted windows gave it a mysterious air and Damien deliberately drove slowly so that people could stare and try to see who was inside.

A voice from the back made him jump: 'Come on, Damien, get your foot down. We've got a busy day today.'

Thompson sat back again. He lit one of his favourite Cuban cigars, a Montecristo No 5, and took a long, satisfying drag.

'Where are we off to?' Damien wanted to know.

Thompson was stroking a baseball bat which he rarely let out of his sight. He loved the sound of bones splintering; it was just like the noise walnuts made when they were forced open by nutcrackers, and it was a noise he'd heard a lot in the past few weeks. His favourite was the patella: as the largest sesamoid bone in the body, the kneecap usually made the loudest and most satisfying crunch which was inevitably followed by a cry of excruciating pain from the victim.

'Damien, have you ever thought about getting involved in education?'

'What, me? I never got no GCSEs at school, so I ain't cut out for all that stuff.'

'You'll be all right with this. You and me are going to teach someone a lesson.'

They pulled up on a main road and walked along two streets to the back of a convenience store. They waited in an alleyway which stank of urine and stale food.

Earlier that day Thompson had made a phone call, feigning to set up a deal to buy skunk. He thought the idiot on the other end was simply too anxious to do business.

Ten minutes later a scruffy-looking man in his late twenties walked in their direction. He was wearing low-slung jeans, a grey hoodie and a baseball cap covered by a huge pair of headphones.

He gulped when Thompson and Henderson blocked his way; his hands became clammy, his mouth dried and fear almost took away his ability to speak.

'Wh-what do you want?' he uttered as Thompson tapped his baseball bat on his palm.

'Well, if it isn't Hayden Wood, the man with sore toes.'

'M-my toes aren't sore . . .'

'I say they are. That's because you're too big for your boots.'

'D-do I know you?'

'Let's just say I'm from the RSPCA – the organisation that looks after animals. I hear you don't like dogs.'

'Who told you that? I love 'em.'

'Not what I've heard. You've been a bit reckless. You really ought to be more careful. You see, an old mate of mine has just lost his best friend. His poor dog was electrocuted. He just went to cock his leg up outside a shop and the shutters were "live". Killed the mutt outright. Now, I hear that was your shop.'

A chilling wind whipped along the alleyway. But sweat was pouring off Woods' back.

'Not me. It wasn't my place. Honest.'

'Don't try to wheedle your way out of this. You thought it was a good idea to stop prying eyes finding out what was going on inside there. But you don't know much about electricity, do you? And because of that you've got blood on your hands.

'I've sussed your game. So too will anybody else with a reasonable sense of smell. Now you're going to get rid of all the cannabis plants that are growing upstairs in that shop, aren't you? Your propagators too. And the lamps. Your customers will be disappointed, so you can send them to me. This is just a taster of what will happen if you don't do as you're told.'

Woods' ear-bursting screams could be heard several streets away. Anyone of a nervous disposition could have been permanently damaged by the sound. But no one dared to get involved; no one dialled 999.

21

The atmosphere in the Derby Storm arena during the day was totally different from game night. Before, during and after a game there was a buzz, excitement and expectation. The exhilaration of victory or the deflation that followed defeat were replaced in the starkness of the day by the unpleasant smell of sweat, the bellowing of precise instructions and the annoying squeak of basketball boots on the parquet floor.

Davies was tempted to head for his usual seat but decided to watch from the end line where he could get a closer look at the players.

'Sorry, this is a closed practice.' The voice, from an assistant coach wearing sweat pants and a Storm top, startled Davies who instantly took out his warrant card.

'Oh, I'll let coach Ross know you're here.'

'No, don't bother. I won't get in the way. Makes a change to see what goes on behind the scenes. It'll allow me to appreciate the game more when I see it for real.'

As it was only a matter of hours after the Storm's defeat to Sheffield, Jason Ross didn't work his team hard for the next half hour. A couple of players who were keen to join the Storm were on trial; Ross took them through a few plays to see how quickly they could pick them up. Then the coach announced the session was over.

'Some of you have got school visits this afternoon. I've just had an email from a group of youngsters we went to see last week. They say they're delighted that we get out into the community to meet with them. Just remember that these young kids idolise professional basketball players like yourselves. The rest of you can take the afternoon off.'

The team got into a huddle, arms raised and all touching as they shouted 'Storm!' on a signal from the team captain.

As they trooped off Davies sidled up to Yandel Eliot and took him out of the gym into a sparse but functional bar. Davies introduced himself; Eliot took a step back on discovering the DI's identity.

'Hey, man, what's this all about?'

'I'm investigating the murder of a reporter, Kevin Michaels. Worked on the East Midlands Express. He suffered some nasty injuries. Had to be someone big and strong to do it. Someone like yourself.'

Eliot, an imposing figure as he looked down at Davies, shrank a fraction of an inch when he heard the word *murder*.

'You can't think I had anything to do with it? I didn't even know the guy.'

'Really. Don't you ever read the papers?'

'No, man, don't look at them.'

Davies produced a copy of Michaels' story hinting at a scandal involving Eliot.

'So you're telling me you've not seen this article? It made the digital edition as well as the printed version.'

'It's a new one on me.'

'And you've never noticed Kevin Michaels at a Storm game? He's here most of the time. Look at this picture – closely.'

Eliot took the photograph, trying to think what to say to get rid of Davies.

'Oh, I've seen him a couple of times. Spoken to him. Said "hi", "what's up", stuff like that. But I've never read a thing that he's written.'

'What were your movements two nights ago – were you anywhere near Heage Lane at Etwall?'

'Where? Never heard of it. Two nights ago? Oh, Rick and I were in Nottingham.'

Before Eliot could continue, a deep, bold, brash voice took him by surprise.

'What the hell's going on here?'

Davies realised this was a different coach Ross to the one he'd heard at the end of the training session. The detective stood his ground and brandished his warrant card. Ross backed off.

'Okay, big fella,' Davies said. 'That's all – for now. I may send one of my officers here later to take a statement from you.'

Eliot walked out of the room. Ross went to follow him.

'Hang on, coach. Need to ask you a couple of questions.'

Ross changed his tone completely as he realised the folly of getting on the wrong side of the law.

'Delighted to help the police in this great country of yours. Now, what would you like to know?'

Davies looked straight into Ross' green, searing eyes.

'Coach, I'm a bit of a basketball fan. I wouldn't call myself an expert, but it doesn't take a genius to realise that Eliot should be playing at a higher level than in England. So why's he here? Anything to do with problems he had back home?'

Ross stroked his thick, dark hair back into place. He had the smugness of a man who considered his career was heading in the right direction. He couldn't have had a wider smile if he'd won the EuroMillions jackpot.

'I've been around this game all my life. It's changed. A lot. That's down to the players. I don't see the mental toughness I once saw in young people. Players don't understand how to win.

'But look at Yandel. He's got a spark in his eye and fire in his belly. He wants to win. He knows how to win. He goes out every night and gives everything he's got.

'I don't care about his past. I'm just grateful that he's here, playing for me. I know he's the right fit for this team. I'd be a happy man if I'd got ten players with the work ethic and fundamental skills that Yandel Eliot's got. He's a winner. Period.'

'Except when he tries a last-second dunk against Sheffield.'

'That was unfortunate. Yes, it cost us the game. But he'll come back stronger after that. Next time a game's on the line, he'll deliver.'

Davies went back into the gym where Parker was shooting hoops. He was the only member of the team still on the court.

'What's up?' he asked. Davies explained about Michaels' death. He again took out a photograph of the dead man.

'I'm sorry to inform you, detective, I don't recall seeing this man. I'm afraid I can't help you.'

Davies wondered if he was telling the truth. Could he be covering up for his colleague?

Davies wanted to know why Parker and Eliot had gone out in Nottingham rather than closer to home.

'A couple of reasons,' said Parker. 'Few people know us in Nottingham, so there's not much chance that coach Ross will get to hear what we've been up to. He doesn't like his players drinking before a game. It doesn't bother me but Yandel likes to unwind with a couple of beers. Nothing wrong with that, is there?'

'And the second reason?'

'Before we came to this country Nottingham's reputation had already reached us. Three things we knew about the city: Robin Hood of course, the fact that the girls there are really beautiful, and there are far more of them than guys. We've definitely found that to be true!'

22

Detective Superintendent Holland, a stern look distorting his face, intercepted Davies.

'What have you got on Bailey?'

Davies kept a straight face, inwardly delighted that the press conference had backfired on Holland. Opening a file, Davies read from a computer printout.

'Only one conviction: drink-driving five years ago. Disqualified from driving for two years. So drunk he didn't know what he was doing. Threatened the arresting officer. Not physically – said he'd do an exposé on him in a national newspaper. It rebounded on him though. Several papers reported it and he lost his job.

'He's worked all over. Never stayed in one place more than three or four years. Likes the booze too much.'

Davies closed the file and passed it to Holland.

'He did work for a while in Cornwall several years ago. A friend of mine's on the force there. Just had a chat with him. Had a problem with Bailey – kept turning up at major incidents almost before the police did. Apparently he used to sit in his office with a high-powered radio listening to a channel broadcasting the two-way communication between the control room and officers.

'He was given a warning. He was simply being a bit too enthusiastic in trying to get a story before the opposition.'

Holland leaned back, deep in thought.

'Right, I suppose there's not a lot we can do about him at the moment. But keep tabs on him. If he even puts a toe out of line, throw the book at him.'

West stopped Davies before he could go into his office: 'Uniform have just picked up Felicity Strutt's husband. They'll be here shortly.'

'Good. You and I will talk to him. The detective super thinks Woodcock's responsible for his wife's disappearance. But I'm not so sure. Let's see what he's got to say, then we can give him a hard time if we need to.'

Rob Woodcock's eyes were fixed on the floor as he trudged into the police station.

He was taken into a modest, clinical, uninviting space. A sign outside Interview Room Number Three lit up: 'Room in use'. There was a table, a few uncomfortable chairs and recording equipment.

When Davies and West came into the room, Woodcock jumped to his feet, panic giving his face an almost grotesque look.

'It's Felicity, isn't it? You've found her!' The words rattled out like a machine gun, his arms, legs and neck tensing in anticipation.

'I'm afraid there's no news at the moment. Sit down, please, Mr Woodcock.' Davies tried to sound as reassuring as possible.

'If you haven't found her, why am I here? Am I under arrest?'

'No, you're not. You're free to leave at any time. We'd just like to ask you a few more questions.'

'But I've told you everything I know.'

'Really?' chipped in West. He flicked through a pile of papers and brought out a witness statement. 'We've been talking to one of your neighbours. Reckons the night before your wife disappeared you had a blazing row.'

'I bet it was that cow at number four. She's had it in for me ever since I reported her to you lot when she had a party. Belting out loud music until five in the morning. I wouldn't believe a word she says.'

'It doesn't matter who told us. You and Felicity did have a row, didn't you?'

'Yes, we did. But it was no worse than any of the arguments we have from time to time. Like most married couples.'

Davies thought about the disagreements he'd had with Lorraine when they'd been together.

'But not all married couples threaten each other.' Another pause as Davies looked slowly and deliberately for the relevant paragraph of the statement.

'You were heard to say "do that and you're a dead woman". You don't deny saying that, do you?'

110

'No, but it wasn't like that,' Woodcock protested. 'I didn't mean I'd kill her.'

'Mr Woodcock, I've been in this job for several years. It wouldn't be the first time someone sitting where you are claimed to be innocent only for us to find out later they'd been telling a pack of lies.'

Woodcock looked Davies in the eye and his voice maintained a level tone. 'How many times do I have to tell you – I love my wife. I'd never do anything to hurt her.'

West increased the tension in the interview room's stifling atmosphere: 'Do you understand that threatening to kill is a criminal offence? Punishable by up to ten years in prison.'

Woodcock sank back into his chair. 'Look, we had an argument. After our first row we decided we needed a trigger, something to demonstrate that one of us has gone too far.

'When Felicity said she would burn my Forest season ticket if she couldn't get her own way, I wasn't having that. So I said, "do that and you're dead". She's said it to me when we've had a row but she never means it.'

'Sounds to me as though you have your fair share of arguments,' West countered.

'Why didn't you tell us this before?' Davies asked.

'Because it makes us sound daft. Go on, admit it. We sound a right stupid couple, don't we? But that's how we talk when we're together. The only "crime" we've committed, if you can call it that, is making too much of a racket so that some interfering busybody heard what we were up to and came to the wrong conclusion.'

Davies got up and started to walk out of the room. 'Let me give you some advice, Mr Woodcock: keep the noise down when you're at home. And close your windows too.'

23

Roger Stone was one of those people you liked or disliked within minutes of meeting him. No one questioned his qualities as a businessman or an entrepreneur. He was the founder of a healthcare company which employed some of the East Midlands' leading scientists who were paid handsomely for their work. It meant he quickly amassed a personal fortune totalling several million pounds.

He was a shrewd judge of character and gave jobs to people who were good decision makers and revelled in the responsibility he gave them. This meant he was able to stand for election to the European Parliament. When he won an East Midlands seat on an unexpected surge of popularity for the Conservatives, he knew his company would be in safe hands while he was away haranguing EU diplomats over some of the ridiculous directives they tried to impose on the electorate.

When British MEPs left the European Parliament after Brexit, Stone was out of politics for only a couple of months before he gained a Westminster seat at a bye-election, his popularity proving decisive at a time when the Tories' appeal was waning.

Stone's success in both business and politics gave him a cavalier attitude which was never more prevalent than in his dealings with women. Initially they noticed his designer suits, immaculately styled hair and tanned complexion – but before too long his leering eyes left them in no doubt about his intentions. They quickly grew tired of his suggestive remarks and his trademark taps on the bottom.

Women who worked for him in both his company and his constituency office tried to fend off his attentions – but most of them were in two minds about leaving his employ because they were paid really well and there were long periods when they were left alone because Stone was away on parliamentary business.

They felt guilty that they weren't doing their bit for women and the #MeToo movement by taking out an assault charge on Stone – but there was little point in strangling the goose that laid the golden egg. A case for constructive dismissal might not lead to much in the way of compensation; anyone undertaking that course of action might struggle to get another job with similar remuneration.

Stone got up from his desk and moved to an adjoining room which was occupied by his constituency office secretary. With a twinkle in his eye he chirped: 'Anna, cancel my engagements for this evening. Something's come up. And something else might do too, if you're lucky.'

Anna, who'd worked for Stone for several years, was accustomed to his salacious remarks and ignored the suggestions.

'But you've got important constituency business this evening. What's the chairman going to say?'

'He can say what he likes. He's not going to get too stressed out – he only needs to think about the size of my majority. As I've often told him, size counts.'

'You're putting me in an impossible position.'

'No, I'm not. But I'd certainly like to.'

'Can't you take anything seriously?'

'Of course I can. Like the business I've got on this evening. There's only one thing that would stop me going to it – and that's a call from the Prime Minister.'

His researcher Richard Turner, hidden behind the door of his own office, heard every word. What was Stone up to now? Was another dodgy business deal in the offing? What was so important that Stone could call off a meeting with his chairman at such short notice?

Rick Parker closed his Bible and placed it carefully in the centre of the coffee table that dominated the living room of his apartment. He liked to start every day by reading a couple of passages from the Good Book and he always ensured it retained a prominent position so that it would be one of the first things visitors saw when entering the room.

He wished more people would come to his new, adopted home. He'd become a good cook over the past few years but, apart from teammates and a couple of supporters who'd put themselves out to make him welcome in Derby, he rarely got the chance to demonstrate his culinary skills.

That was often why his compatriot Yandel Eliot was the guinea pig whenever Parker discovered a new recipe that he wanted to try out.

The two were complete opposites yet that was one of the reasons why Parker thought they got on so well. Eliot was extrovert and exuberant while Parker was introverted and introspective. Eliot lived for the moment; Parker planned out his life and was already thinking about what he was going to do after he finished playing basketball.

Parker respected Eliot's talents on the basketball court, realising the big man had the ability to drive a crowd wild with his trademark allez-oop dunks and strength around the basket. Eliot appreciated how Parker could take over a game, his vision in spotting an open teammate matched by his success at shooting from long range.

Parker, a non-drinker who swore only occasionally and put others before himself, wanted to reach out and help Eliot with his off-court problems. At the same time Parker knew he couldn't dictate how Eliot led his life: the point guard could keep an eye on his colleague but if Eliot wanted to adopt a non-Christian attitude, there was little Parker could do about it.

He decided the best way to help Eliot was to spend as much time with him as possible. Parker wasn't a big fan of going to bars and clubs – but that was where Eliot enjoyed himself immensely. He also liked to drink a lot. Parker knew that could lead to trouble; but if he were alongside Eliot, he might be able to prevent him from doing anything reckless.

To an outsider, it might seem odd that less than 24 hours before a game a professional athlete like Eliot would drink to excess. Parker had tackled him about it when they were on their own.

'It's just something I have to do, man. The last time I didn't drink the night before a game, I was shit. Couldn't rebound a damn thing. I was out of my head before the next game and, man, I was awesome! Had a triple double, the only time I've ever done that. Now that's how I always prepare for a ball game. But don't tell the coach – he'd have me on a plane back to the States in no time.'

When his sporting career was over, Parker thought he might like to go into counselling work. He was fascinated by trying to find out what made people tick. Eliot was a good case study; Parker could learn a tremendous amount by staying close to his teammate.

24

Anyone getting a glimpse of the articulated trailer on an isolated farm wouldn't have bothered to take a second look. It had no distinguishing marks and it didn't seem out of place alongside machinery whose prominent feature was rust.

Davies turned off a narrow road onto a farm track, driving slowly so as not to damage his car on the uneven, rutted surface. He stopped near the trailer, careful to avoid mud patches caused by the recent torrential rain. He hoped he wouldn't need a push to get his car going again later.

He tapped on the trailer and a door opened within seconds.

'Hello, Miles, come on in.'

Davies coughed as a pungent, musky, sweet, piney smell went straight through his nostrils into his chest. He gasped and his hand shot up to cover his nose.

'Bloody hell, Scott, I feel high just coming in here. How on earth do you stand it?'

'You get used to it after a while.'

Scott Dixon was in charge of the East Midlands Police Drug Reduction Action Management programme, otherwise known as DRAM.

The trailer had racks from ceiling to floor with bags containing cannabis, cocaine and other substances. They'd been destined for drug dealers across the Midlands; Dixon requisitioned samples for analysis as the force battled to stay one step ahead of the criminals. It was a war that some officers felt they couldn't win – as soon as they got a drug dealer off the streets, someone else took over.

Dixon's grey hair hung over his collar and covered his ears. His beard, mainly grey apart from a couple of black spots near his chin, needed a trim. He resembled a homeless alcoholic rather than a police officer.

'Good to see you, Miles – been a long time.'

Dixon and Davies began their police careers at the same time. They shared experiences and supported each other through their fledgling, difficult years. But promotions and an increasing workload meant they had little time to get together socially.

'You're still busy then,' Davies said, casting an eye around the trailer which would be ecstasy to a drug-taker in more ways than one.

'You'd better believe it. We're uncovering a cannabis farm virtually every day. And the gangs are becoming more and more sophisticated.'

'In what way?'

'Getting a pack of vicious dogs to guard their stash. Disguising the entrance to wherever they're keeping the stuff with a kennel. I've even heard some growers are going underground. They're always thinking of new ways to keep us off the scent, as it were.'

He laughed when he realised the pun.

'We're still a new unit and we haven't got a big enough team. But you know all about that. Anyway, what can I do for you?'

Davies stopped looking at a small press used for crushing cannabis into small blocks.

'Kevin Michaels. Did you know him?'

'The reporter who was murdered? Came across him a couple of times. Didn't have much to do with him. He called me a few days ago. Said he wanted to have a chat. Something about a story he was researching. I arranged to meet him in a pub.'

'And . . . ?'

'He never showed up. The following morning your lot found him dead.'

25

Keith Holland beamed as he greeted Roger Stone, his handshake as firm as if he were grabbing a criminal by the throat. The MP gripped the detective superintendent's hand with a similar amount of gusto.

'Keith, glad you could make it.'

'No problem. I was over here anyway checking on a couple of investigations. Good choice, this – I don't think anyone knows us here.'

They met in a hotel in Leicester that was part of a chain and was similar to every other branch in every town and city in the UK.

They ordered drinks, Stone opting for a whisky and soda while Holland plumped for a gin and tonic. The chink as they toasted each other's health reverberated around the near-empty bar.

'You've been a bit busy, haven't you?' Stone had a broad smile which lit up his face.

'You could say that. It's non-stop at the moment.'

'I'm intrigued. A newspaper reporter dead. A weathergirl missing. Are the cases linked?'

'Not sure.'

Stone had a mischievous look in his eye.

'Haven't you got enough staff to solve those crimes? The police and crime commissioner hasn't made that many cuts!'

Holland gazed at his drink. 'The problem is the guy who's running the investigations doesn't know what he's doing. I'm just waiting for him to make a balls-up, then I can get rid of him.'

Stone called the barman over, jabbed a finger at his and Holland's glasses and indicated he wanted refills.

'Now, Keith, what's going on with our care homes? Those reports on the TV haven't done us any good at all. We stand to lose thousands. Might have to offload a few of them.'

'Just sit tight. Short-term pain, long-term gain. I've got everything in hand.'

'Who is this guy Bailey? How did he manage to find out so much?'

'I'm not sure. He's got a big nose. Likes poking it in other people's business. He tried to get some dirt on you, didn't he?'

Stone slugged back his whisky as though it were a soft drink.

'What, you mean the cash-for-laws case?'

'Yeah. What was all that about?'

'When I was in the European Parliament a couple of journalists from a foreign TV channel thought they could get me to admit that I'd accepted money in exchange for tabling amendments in Brussels. But I was too smart for them. Saw it coming a mile off. It goes on quite a lot these days. You've probably heard about programmes like *Dispatches* on Channel 4 and *Panorama*. Get journalists to pretend to be lobbyists.

122

They're even doing it in countries like Bulgaria and Romania. But there was no way I was ever going to fall for it.

'Bailey thought he would do his own digging to try and get the story. Probably thinks he's a better journalist than he really is. He got no further than the foreigners did.'

Holland noticed the smug look on Stone's face. The detective superintendent swirled his drink, making the ice cubes clank against the side of the glass, before taking a sip.

'Just be careful,' said Holland. 'There are all sorts of people who'd like you to slip up. I don't want you having to resign from Westminster. You've only just got your feet under the table.'

'There's no chance of that. Anyway, you've got more pressing things to think about – Gordon Bailey, for one.'

'Don't worry about him. He won't be getting in our way again.'

26

Davies told the team about Michaels' aborted meeting with Scott Dixon, then information from Mark Roberts gave him a feeling that the investigation was finally making progress.

'We thought we might have a few problems getting hold of CCTV because it's such an isolated area. There's an old people's home but their cameras don't show the road going past the building, and the area's mainly agricultural.

'But that could have worked in our favour. Remember a couple of years ago there was a spate of thefts from farms? Thieves were stealing tractors and exporting them to developing countries, then they were nicking telehandlers so that they could steal cash machines from garages and convenience shops.

'There's a farm on Heage Lane that was targeted a couple of times and lost thousands of pounds worth of machinery. The farmer was told his insurance wouldn't be valid if he didn't beef up his security, so he installed a really good CCTV system. Several cameras, the sort that take good pictures. We've got hold of the footage. Just about to start going through it.'

'Great stuff.' Davies was galvanized into action.

'Let's extend the search for Michaels. We must be able to spot him somewhere in the city or beyond. How did he get from the centre to Heage Lane? Did he meet up with anybody on the way? Did he make a detour? Check out all his haunts. He was a journalist – someone in a pub or a coffee shop must have known him. What was his mood like on the day he died? And try to come up with a motive. What's the message the killer was trying to convey with the fountain pen?

'Mark, cold cases – anything resembling Kevin Michaels' murder?'

Roberts thumbed through documents containing yellowing papers that had been handled numerous times over the years.

'Nothing that really matches up. But I've just got an odd feeling about this.'

He handed Davies a file into the death of Robert Campbell, a 28-year-old accountant who'd reported in his spare time on football matches and various events in his community. He'd been murdered twenty years ago.

'Not a journalist as such, said Roberts, 'but a guy who had lots of contacts in newspapers and radio. There was the suspicion that he'd uncovered some incriminating evidence against a council leader although the investigating team couldn't stand that up.'

'Bit of a tenuous link isn't it?' asked Davies.

'Possibly. But there are some weird aspects to this case. The victim was shot dead – there was speculation that it was a contract killing. But after he'd been shot he had a bottle of ink poured down his throat. The ink wouldn't have been enough to poison him, so was the killer trying to send a message in the same way as Michaels' murderer?'

Davies shuddered as he considered this information. Could the killer of Robert Campbell and Kevin Michaels be the same person? Had the killer used a hit man to take out Campbell and later progressed to carrying out his own executions? If he had, why was there so long between murders?

Davies snapped out of his trance-like state. 'What have you got on the missing weather presenter?'

'Boss, we've found her car. Uniform on patrol spotted it in a side street just off Mansfield Road.'

Davies made the connection that it wasn't far from the hotel where Felicity had been spotted. He presumed everyone else noted it too.

'Where's the car now?'

'In the pound. Forensics are all over it.'

'Good. Keep onto them. Maybe that'll give us a lead as to who she was with that night.'

Roberts wasn't finished. 'We've checked the airport – no one by the name of Strutt or Woodcock has booked in on any of the airlines. It's the same with Eurostar, although there's nothing to stop anyone turning up on the day and buying a ticket at the gate, if they've got any seats left. It costs a lot of money to do that – but Felicity would have paid up willingly if she was determined to leave the country.

'As for her mobile, there's been no signal since the evening she went missing. We've got a trace on it so as soon as she turns it back on, we'll know.

'Her social media accounts don't tell us much: ten thousand followers on Twitter, a few thousand on Instagram, fifty-odd friends on Facebook. Her Facebook account is strange – she doesn't post much and she's deleted everything that was on the site before she got the job presenting the weather. Maybe there's something in her past that she doesn't want people to know about.'

Roberts turned to another piece of paper.

'One other thing, boss. I know you ruled out Felicity's husband, but we've found this: Woodcock was a member of an archery club. He got thrown out for what was said to be "inappropriate behaviour". Now that could be anything. Maybe someone ought to have another word with him.'

'Thanks for that, Mark. You're right, "inappropriate" can encompass all sorts of things. Woodcock didn't mention this when James and I spoke to him. I think he's got some explaining to do.'

27

The alarm clock jolted Gordon Bailey out of his slumber – not that he went into a deep sleep very much these days. The alcohol knocked him out shortly after he fell into bed, but then it meant he woke up at regular intervals throughout the early hours. He also had to get out of bed on more than one occasion to empty his bladder.

The jingle which signalled the start of the radio station's news bulletin reminded him that it was a weekday and work was calling him.

He heaved his body towards the edge of the bed, swung his tired legs over the side and with great difficulty sat upright. The room whirred around and refused to stop. Bailey grabbed the sides of his head and tried to take control of his brain – but with little success. None of the news stories registered with him and the presenter was reading out the weather forecast before Bailey dared to stand up.

His head felt full of cotton wool and he lurched from side to side as he made his way to the bathroom. It was as if a drummer were inside his head, thumping out a regular rhythm on a bass drum. His mouth felt as though he'd had nothing to drink for days although he'd consumed a man's recommended weekly intake of alcohol the previous evening.

He grabbed a glass and shoved it under the cold tap. How he wished he'd done the same thing the previous evening and swapped water for wine and whisky.

The two-bedroomed flat wasn't the most sought-after property. It was in the Hyson Green area of Nottingham where back in the 1980s there'd been riots due to racial tension and what was euphemistically described as 'inner-city deprivation'.

But the area which had the largest ethnic minority population in the city had benefited from a huge injection of money. The economy was thriving and people were again enjoying living in Hyson Green, as they did in the 'sixties and 'seventies when it had an enviable community spirit.

It had two Asian supermarkets, book shops, jewellers, general stores and barbers owned by people from India, Pakistan, Bangladesh, Poland, Spain, Iraq, Turkey and other countries.

People who hadn't visited Hyson Green still thought of it as being an unwholesome area but it satisfied Bailey's needs. He didn't spend a lot of time at the flat – he just wanted a comfortable bed where he could get his head down at the end of the day and somewhere quiet on the odd occasion when he had to work from home.

He splashed cold water over his face but it hardly helped to displace his lethargy.

129

His mind wandered to imagine what the day held in store for him. He lurched forwards when he thought the news editor might get him to do a story about Felicity Strutt. Why would the station bother to do anything about her yet? There was no indication she'd come to any harm, so it didn't make sense to run a piece at this stage, did it? But it wouldn't be the first time the station had covered something with dubious news value.

Bailey was hoping for something good to get his teeth into. He'd got a couple of things he was investigating, but there were occasions when he wasn't allowed to work on them because he was needed to produce a report to fill that evening's programme.

The warm water cascaded down his body when he decided after all to take a shower. The smell of sticky sweat and stale alcohol started to evaporate; he was beginning to think more clearly.

He deserved to cover the best stories, didn't he? He had a great record, everyone knew that. As a young reporter, wasn't he the one who uncovered a major sex scandal that involved judges, police chiefs and even government ministers? His newspaper would have had the story published if Special Branch officers hadn't gone to his office, held him against a wall and threatened him with prison if he didn't hand over his notes and research. He was naive then, admittedly, and hadn't photocopied the relevant material. Now, whenever he got a whiff of a decent story, he made sure he had several copies in different digital formats; he'd never make that mistake again.

Hadn't he produced exclusive after exclusive, everything from a drugs ring involving a former football legend to a story about councillors taking part in lurid sex sessions on a foreign junket?

He was an old-school journalist, and there weren't many around like him these days. Today's reporters were shackled to their desk for most of the time – it wasn't original journalism and they wouldn't know a good story if it dropped into their lap. They were always checking social media; they'd even write stories about how people were reacting on Twitter to a news item.

His method was to get out of the office, meet people, talk to them, listen to them. The best place to meet people, he felt, was the pub; getting drunk proved to be a necessary by-product.

He never intended to sup a huge amount of alcohol, but drink loosened uncommunicative people's tongues. And it was disrespectful not to imbibe with them.

He dried himself off and reached into the wardrobe for a clean shirt. The clothes rail was empty. He searched for the shirt he'd worn the previous day, finding it lying on a stool, partially crumpled. He put it on again, chose a different tie – and hoped no one would notice.

Shit, he was going to be late for the morning's prospects meeting at this rate. He hoped the trams were running on time.

28

Miles Davies had his mornings worked out to perfection. A light but nutritious breakfast, a cup of tea while getting dressed and the detective inspector was ready for anything.

This morning he'd even found time to have a quick tidy-up around the house – not that his former railway worker's cottage took too much looking after. The estate agent called it a 'character home' occupying 'an exceptionally convenient position'. The word Davies used was functional. Luxuries were something he simply couldn't afford after a costly break-up with his wife. But he did admit it was in a useful location as it was only seconds from the railway station.

It contained a living room for a less than state-of-the-art television for the odd occasions when he had time to relax, a kitchen that was too small to swing a cat around and three pokey bedrooms, one decked out in blue, the favourite colour of his son who came for a sleepover too infrequently.

He was just about to go out of the door when his phone rang. A picture of his ex-wife Lorraine stared at him from his mobile.

His time with Lorraine had started brilliantly; they seemed ideally suited and before long she became pregnant. Davies turned into a doting dad, always showing off the latest photo of his son Jordan to colleagues at the station.

Davies even accepted Lorraine's daughter from a previous relationship as his own.

But the pressures of the job came between them, just as it affected many couples in which only one was a police officer. Lorraine became tired of spending so much time on her own and found comfort in the arms of a keyboard player in a group who were playing in a nearby pub.

Despite that Davies harboured visions of getting back together with Lorraine. For the first and only time in his life he'd felt a failure. It was a feeling that stuck with him all these months later.

He'd agreed to a quick divorce, gave Lorraine everything she asked for and threw himself even deeper into his work while he thought about how he could win her back.

'Good morning, Lorraine. I was just about to leave for work.'

Her voice sounded concerned, apologetic even. 'Oh, I'm sorry. I should have thought about the time. I'll make it quick. How are you, okay?'

Davies hesitated. Her tone took him by surprise.

'I'm fine, thanks. You?'

'I'm good.'

'How about Jordan?'

'He's good too. In fact that's why I'm ringing.'

Davies's heart rate quickened as he wondered what was coming. Did she want to move away, take him somewhere so that the new man in her life could get to know him better and Jordan would begin to forget about his natural father?

'Can you look after him on Sunday? We've organised a surprise party for my dad. It's his sixty-fifth birthday. You know he doesn't like any fuss. We weren't going to do anything but we've decided we can't let this go by without marking it, so we're having a small celebration.'

Davies liked Lorraine's dad. He was a gentle, straightforward man who always had time for others.

She went on: 'It's such a long way down to Kent. I've managed to get Monday off. I think it would be better for Jordan to have a good night's sleep. He's at school the next morning, so I don't think it's fair for him to be out till all hours. Will you have him?'

'Of course. And I'll take him to school on Monday.'

'That's great. Thanks. You don't think there's any chance that you'll be called into work, do you?'

'No. I think Jordan's a bit too young to be chasing after criminals, so I'll definitely take the day off. I'm owed some leave.'

'I hope you have a lovely time together.'

Davies knew the Storm had a rare Sunday afternoon game. He was determined it would be the first time Jordan, who'd started to take an interest in basketball, would see a live game.

Lorraine then told Davies everything she'd been doing for the past few weeks despite saying the call would be brief. He resisted the temptation to say 'I know, I've seen most of it on Facebook' before she ended the call.

He felt an inner glow and there was a spring in his step as he marched up the street. He thought about the traffic building up on the A52 towards Nottingham. It was already the rush hour. He wondered: why do they call it that? Nobody rushes and it lasts far longer than an hour. It was one of those days he was glad he lived so close to the railway station.

29

Half an hour later Davies was in Nottingham. He walked along platform five, up a footbridge and headed towards the tram stop.

Construction workers were already on site nearby, the noise of drilling, boring and tunnelling adding to the sounds of lorries and buses forcing their way through the city.

Davies looked up: the ubiquitous cranes signalled that yet more renovation was going on to try to turn Nottingham into the most important place in the East Midlands. But he couldn't get out of his head images of the fighting machines in Jeff Wayne's *War of the Worlds*. Worth a listen to later, he thought as he stepped onto the crowded tram and found just enough room to stand in a corner.

After arriving at the station he called the morning meeting to order. Mark Roberts was keen to take the floor and update everyone on his findings.

'This is CCTV from a farm on Heage Lane, close to where Kevin Michaels' body was found. We've had the footage enhanced and while we can't make out any facial features, this shows us one important attribute of the man who could well be the killer: he's really tall.

'You can just spot him getting out of his car and going round to the passenger side. You can't make out much more than that – you can't tell if there's anyone else in the car or if he drags anyone along the road. But why would he stop on a country road at that time of night?'

'Great work, Mark. Make of car – any idea?'

'A few people with more knowledge of cars than me have taken a look at it. Reckon it's a BMW.'

'So we've got a really big guy in a what could possibly be a BMW. Check how many BMWs have been stolen in the past week or so.

'And who is this guy? We need to identify him. Check the national database – see how many tall people there are in the Midlands. Let's go for everyone above, say, six feet five to start with.

'Anybody else got any ideas?'

'Isn't there a group for tall people, a sort of lonely-hearts club so they don't have to carry a stepladder around when they go on a date?' Paul Allen's comment raised a titter around the incident room.

'I'm serious. I used to know a lad at school who shot up when he was a teenager. I mean physically, nothing to do with drugs. All his so-called mates would laugh at him. Made silly comments, like "is it cold up there?" No girl would go out with him because they just weren't on the same level.'

His colleagues groaned. Davies asked him to check it out.

'How about sportsmen?' asked West. 'Didn't the cricket club sign someone a couple of years ago, a fast bowler, who was a bit of a giant?'

'Don't forget rowers,' Allen chipped in. 'Wasn't there a big lad in the Boat Race last year? About six foot ten. There could be someone that tall at one of the local rowing clubs. And tennis players. There was a huge South African who did well at Wimbledon a couple of years ago too.'

'You're right,' said Davies. 'We'd better find out how many more big guys there are who fit the description. See what you can come up with for the next briefing.'

30

Her body shuddered as she awoke, an indistinguishable thud jolting her out of a deep sleep.

The thick, lined curtains blocked out any light, so it was impossible for her to know whether it was day or night.

She heard something against the windowpane. A bird that had lost its bearings and crashed into it? Someone breaking in who'd managed to discover she was being held captive and wanted to inflict more suffering on her? Hadn't she been through enough already?

Then: whistling. She concentrated on the sound, wide awake now, trying to make sense of what was happening outside her prison.

She thought she recognised the tune. The whistler was off-key and kept taking breaths in the wrong places but, yes, she'd got it: Always Look on the Bright Side of Life. *How ironic. What film was it from? She couldn't remember – she wasn't born when it was released. Didn't matter. She'd identified it. But who was the whistler? And what was he doing?*

The staccato sound continued, interspersed with thuds followed by a squeaking noise as cloth met glass.

A window cleaner! It must be daylight and it can't be raining, she concluded, although knowledge of the day's weather wasn't much use to her.

She recalled fairy tales from her childhood, a princess locked in a tower, a damsel in distress waiting for the handsome prince to pull off a daring rescue. Was the window cleaner fit, fantastic and fanciable?

'Help!' she shrieked. She'd forgotten about the tape keeping her lips together which ensured her anguished cry came out as a whimper. Panicking now, she pursed her lips and emitted another cry that was about as loud as a ticking clock.

She slumped back, her optimism about being released evaporating more quickly than butter when it's left out in the sun.

The whistling continued but became quieter. She pictured the window cleaner climbing down his ladder, unaware of how he'd missed the opportunity to become a lifesaver.

Davies was about to sample his first coffee of the day when West interrupted.

'Boss, we've had a call from a woman who works for a charity, tries to prevent young kids from being sexually exploited. Reckons she ran into Kevin Michaels earlier in the evening before he was found dead. Could have been the last person to see him alive. Apart from his killer.'

'Okay, grab your coat. You can get the drinks in later.'

There was nothing remarkable about the charity's offices: too opulent and it might have put off anyone who'd suffered a life-changing sexual encounter from telling their story, too untidy and it could have had a similar effect.

Davies and West sat down and took in the surroundings. A couple of spider plants, a standard lamp with a low glow and a coffee table with a variety of well-thumbed magazines gave what was effectively an interview room a homely feel.

Kath Harper was in her late thirties and was wearing a cream blouse and dark skirt. Her blonde hair, cut well and parted down the middle, fell over her shoulders. She had an air of gentle efficiency. But Davies noticed that behind her dark-framed glasses there was a sadness in her eyes which were red through crying.

Her neck and shoulders were hunched up as she perched on the edge of a chair opposite the two detectives.

Her voice was close to breaking. Davies expected her to start crying again at any moment.

'What happened the last time you saw Kevin?' he said with as much compassion as he could muster.

'I ran into Kevin by accident. I'd been to give a talk to a community group in the city and I was going back to my car.

'Kevin was coming towards me. I stopped and said hello. He seemed in a hurry and didn't want to talk.

'I said I wouldn't keep him long and just wanted to thank him for all he'd done for the charity.'

'So what had he done?' Davies smiled, hoping she'd keep herself together for a little longer.

'He was doing all sorts of fundraising. Organising raffles, jumble sales. He even got a friend of his to run the Robin Hood Marathon.

That raised several thousand pounds for us. Then of course there was the publicity he managed to get for us in the paper.

'As a charity, we're always looking to expand. But to do that we have to keep raising money. Kevin realised that and he was a godsend, so I just wanted to tell him how much we appreciated what he was doing for us.

'He was normally so friendly, so . . . approachable. But not on that evening.'

She stopped, looked out of the window and then at the ceiling.

'What time was this?' Davies prompted.

'Must have been, what, about nine o'clock?'

'Have you any idea why he appeared different?'

'He just seemed preoccupied. He said "thanks" a couple of times and "it's nothing". He just wanted to get away. Very unusual.'

'And what was the last thing he said to you?'

She could hardly speak: 'His last words to me were "I'll see you soon".'

31

The rain clattered against the rotting windowpane, barely enough paint on it to indicate what colour it should be if it had had only an infinitesimal amount of maintenance. The noise was loud enough to waken even the heaviest sleeper. The old man was cocooned in a pile of sheets and blankets. He could afford only to eat in his draughty, basic house – he couldn't heat it as well.

A slurping sound and saliva dripping off his cheek alerted him to the fact that he couldn't put off getting up any longer.

When he'd brought the dog home, he thought the animal would be good company, a friend to give him unconditional love. Sure enough, the border collie-greyhound cross did love his new master whose house was far better than his two previous homes – the first where a family treated him abominably and the second an underfunded rescue centre. But he was a creature of habit and needed his exercise.

The old man crawled out of bed and threw on the clothes he'd worn the previous day. He staggered downstairs, gripping the handrail and putting one foot next to the other in the same way a young child who'd just learned to walk would negotiate stairs.

After a couple of minutes he shivered as his foot stomped down on the last step. Pausing to regain his breath, he slipped the fraying, grubby lead off its hook, ensured he had enough poop scoop bags in his pocket and went for the first of three obligatory daily walks with his best friend.

Within seconds the unrelenting rain permeated his coat, pullover and trousers and dripped off his glasses. His light grey, thinning hair stuck to his scalp as he squelched along a street that was struggling to cope with the deluge.

He squeezed out a 'good morning' to a couple of other dog owners, people he would have ignored if they hadn't also been forced out by their animals into the early-morning blackness. Otherwise the streets were bare, apart from a couple of shift workers' cars which gingerly passed through deepening puddles.

The old man's tatty shoes gave him less protection than a pair of threadbare slippers as the inescapable rain bounced off the pavement. His socks felt as though they'd come out of a washing machine without going through a tumble dryer. He let the dog off its lead and considered how the advantages of owning a dog were diminishing now that he'd entered his eighth decade.

Like a toddler escaping the attention of a parent, the dog bounded off. Usually he raced back whenever he heard his master call. But not this time.

The septuagenarian tried to go faster but his limbs protested; they ached as if he'd walked a hundred miles instead of a few hundred yards. He wished he could summon up some of the energy he used to burn off in his younger days. But now the only things quickening were his heart rate and his wheezing.

Where was the stupid animal?

A couple of minutes later he heard the dog barking, a warning yet protective sound. Hoping the noise wouldn't disturb anyone who was still enjoying a peaceful slumber, the old man panted as he tried to catch up.

He found the dog crouching down, concerned, drawing attention to something inside the Arboretum. The Nottingham park was locked at this time of day in a bid to stop any anti-social behaviour. A nine-foot-high wall deterred anyone who thought they might go in after dark for a bit of fun.

Through the bars of a light green steel fence he could make out what appeared to be a pile of rubbish, possibly the work of a flytipper.

He took off his glasses, wiped away most of the rain and looked again: it was the crumpled shape of a body. The old man gave it a cursory glance, put the lead round the dog's neck and dragged it back along the street.

32

Enthusiastic officers were still fired up to investigate Kevin Michaels' murder and Felicity Strutt's disappearance. But Davies was starting to become concerned about their well-being, realising that the long hours would affect them before too long.

One of the older members of the team took off his reading glasses and addressed the next briefing: 'Boss, we've just had reports of a car being burnt out. Just off the A38, south of Derby. It looks like a BMW. We're getting a forensics team out to check it over. Not much left of it, so we may not be able to get any DNA off it.'

Paul Allen tried to lift the mood. 'I've been in contact with the Tall Persons Club GB and Ireland. Bit of a misnomer, really – you don't have to be a certain height to get in, you just have to consider yourself "taller than average".

'They've not had any organised social events around here in the past couple of months. But the director I spoke to said there was nothing to stop any of their members arranging their own trips here. Obviously they've heard about Nottingham's reputation for its nightlife, so any of them could have come here under their own steam.

'We've found a few people six feet six and over in the East Midlands. We're getting uniform to pay them a visit.

'No tall cricketers in the patch. Notts had one but he's in Australia for the winter.

'Couple of big rugby players are on the list – Leicester Tigers have got one, a second-row forward, Nottingham have got another. We're looking into their movements too.

'No rowers, though. At least, no one above six feet four.'

Davies was suddenly aware of Detective Superintendent Holland standing at the back of the room.

'Isn't there another sport you should be looking at, Miles? Don't you follow that ridiculous sport basketball? I'm told you can't get a game unless you're a bit of a giant. Have you looked into the local teams yet?'

Davies looked hard at Holland. 'I've got that in hand.'

'I saw a picture in the paper of someone from – who was it, Derby Storm? – the other day. Those teal uniforms – they make you look more like a bus driver than a basketball player. I thought he worked for the council.' He grinned but no one followed suit.

'And what about Felicity Strutt. Have you actually made any progress yet?'

Before he could answer a uniformed officer, out of breath after running up a couple of flights of stairs, barged in.

'Boss, sorry – I've been told to let you know: we've got an attempt murder.'

Opened in 1852, the Arboretum was the first public park in Nottingham. It was designed to house a wide variety of trees, having no fewer than sixty different species. It was also a place to relax yet was only minutes from the city centre.

Davies left his car at the top end of the park, on Arboretum Street, and within seconds of getting out his thick, brown hair stuck to his head, rain dripped into his eyes and his raincoat turned a darker, deeper colour.

He approached a uniformed officer who looked deflated after being chosen to stand guard over the crime scene. He'd have preferred wading through masses of paperwork in the police station rather than being out in this miserable weather. He made a note of Davies' name and lifted the blue-and-white tape, allowing him through the gates which had been pushed open. Just over to the left a white tent had already been set up.

Wise move, Davies thought, especially as the residential area was home to a girls' high school and a day nursery. Didn't want anyone from there getting hysterical about what had happened on their doorstep.

Davies pulled up his collar and hunched his shoulders. Lightning flashed in the distance. Thunder boomed across the city, a haunting echo that reverberated seconds after the initial clap.

Davies thought it hadn't been warm enough for thunder. Or was that an old wives' tale? It would be something he could take up with Felicity Strutt, if his team ever found her.

A detective who was one of the first on the scene wiped his forehead with the back of his hand. He was formally dressed but had on a long waterproof and wellingtons.

'Morning, sir.'

'Morning. What have we got?'

'White male, probably late fifties or early sixties. Somebody's given him a good beating. No sign of locks being smashed or gates being opened.'

Davies noticed similarities between Kevin Michaels' murder and the attack on this man.

'Who found him?'

'A man walking his dog. That's him over there.'

He pointed to a sad old man, the rain pouring onto his frail body and making him look smaller than his true height. His eyes stared into the distance, a sense of bemusement and fear rooting him to the spot. A dog sat next to him, his lead slack, a look on his face that seemed to ask what all the fuss was about.

'Sir, it's a bit of a strange one. He reckons he was here not long after it got light. But he didn't actually call us until around eight o'clock – a couple hours after he first saw the victim.'

Davies went up to the pensioner, stroked his dog and introduced himself.

'So, do you walk your dog around here often?'

'Come here most days. First thing in the morning, before the trams start. We go out again later in the day but not here. Gets too busy and I can't let him off his lead.'

'And what time did you get here this morning?'

'He usually wakes me at about half five, so we must have been here not long after six.'

Davies was exasperated by the old man but kept the same soft tone in his voice.

'Why didn't you ring us until eight o'clock? We might have lost vital forensic evidence – it could have been washed away in all this rain.'

'Well, it were obvious the bloke weren't going anywhere. And my dog, he wanted his breakfast . . .'

33

Davies' team were buzzing as they assembled for the next briefing.

'We've got another case to investigate. An attempt murder in the Arboretum. The victim is known to us: Gordon Bailey, television reporter.'

West brought up Bailey's photo which was displayed alongside those of Kevin Michaels and Felicity Strutt.

'There's the possibility that one person might be responsible for the attack on Bailey, the death of Kevin Michaels and the disappearance of Felicity Strutt. James, what do we know about Bailey?'

'Gordon John Bailey. Sixty years old. TV reporter. The initial reports say he was given a good going-over, then it appears someone threw him over the wall into the Arboretum. Latest condition: it's touch and go whether he'll make it.

'Been a bit of a problem in the past, has Mr Bailey. Like some of the old-school hacks you might have come across, he liked a drink. But according to his boss who we've had a quick chat to, he was a damned good reporter. That's how he came to get his last job – someone thought he was worth another chance.'

Davies took over. 'Thanks, James. What we need to know is: what happened before Bailey was found in that park?

'Was he in an argument with someone? Obviously we're going to be heavily reliant on CCTV, so let's check all the cameras in the city centre to get any sightings of him. I know it's a huge job but I'm confident you'll trace his movements.

'At some stage I want the archives at the TV station checked: which major stories had he been working on? Had he offended someone in authority by running a piece that showed them in a bad light? A politician? A business leader? Was he working on any stories that would have been damaging if they'd been broadcast? Maybe someone decided to make sure he didn't get the story on the TV.

'And find out if we can positively link the attacks on Michaels and Bailey, and Felicity Strutt's disappearance. Bailey wasn't a great fan of hers, that's for sure. But maybe he discovered the same thing that she was working on before she vanished. Let's get some answers!'

34

The evening regional news programme went smoothly and professionally. It was the typical, five-minute weekend bulletin that started with a heart-breaking story about a couple who were hoping for justice after their young daughter died in a boating accident in Spain. It continued with a story about a hospital taking steps to ensure it came out of special measures after being criticised for high death rates.

Halfway through the programme the presenter's voice became edgy as she read out a short piece about the attempted murder of Gordon Bailey. Details were sketchy and the police were appealing for witnesses.

In the gallery the director's voice cut through the room; the presenter acknowledged with a respectful silence the instructions about which camera would be used for the next story.

The bank of monitors covered a whole wall of the room which looked full even though there were fewer than half a dozen people in it. Lighting was kept to a minimum, the speakers were on low to discourage anyone from chatting and the air-conditioning system ensured that the only sweat was of the nervous kind.

When the programme had finished the director thanked everyone for their endeavours.

West and Davies again watched from chairs reserved for occasional visitors.

'How on earth do you manage to keep on top of things?' asked an impressed West.

'It's second nature – it comes with practice. All directors start on these shorter bulletins before they work up to a thirty-minute programme. Everyone's done it so many times that the only thing I get worried about is complacency. Mind you, we do plan everything beforehand. If there are live elements, we try to have a rehearsal so that we're not caught unawares.'

'It all looks so slick,' West enthused.

'Thanks. We've got a good team here. It's a great place to work and the atmosphere's really good. Some people have been here for years – they wouldn't even consider going anywhere else. When new staff come in, they usually fit in right from the start. They can't believe how everyone works together and there's no bitchiness. That can be such a problem in other TV stations.'

Davies wanted to take a different line: 'Gordon Bailey. How did he fit in?'

'Surprisingly well. Everyone knows about his problems, but the management were prepared to give him a chance, so we were quite happy to go along with it.'

'What about Chris Watson? He didn't employ Gordon, did he? Did they get on?'

Everyone else had left the gallery. Davies could hear the constant, low drone of electrical equipment as he waited for the reply.

The director was careful with his choice of words. 'Chris tolerated him. He said he would never have employed Gordon if he'd been the boss when Gordon arrived.

'Chris is in a really difficult position. He's under pressure all the time to increase the viewing figures. He was worried that Gordon's drinking would be a problem. Chris usually plays things by the book. He told Gordon he had to watch his step – one mistake and he was out.'

Davies recalled the meeting he and West had had with Bailey. 'Did Gordon get on with Felicity Strutt?'

Another silence. 'As far as I know.'

'That's not what I heard. I was told he couldn't stand the sight of her.'

'Who told you that? As far as I'm concerned, there was never any animosity between them. Why should there be? They passed the time of day when they were both in the newsroom but they hardly ever worked together, so I shouldn't think there was any reason for Gordon to dislike her.'

Davies and West were taken to the newsroom where they questioned the remaining staff. All were united in their shock and fear at the attack on Bailey. He wasn't the most popular figure in the

155

newsroom but, they discovered, Bailey could be generous, warm and friendly when the mood took him. Conversely he could be sharp, sullen and sarcastic when he was struggling to meet a deadline or wasn't making much headway on a story.

Davies was surprised to see Chris Watson in the office on a Saturday. He was comforting staff who were upset about Bailey being in intensive care, reassuring others who were wondering if there'd be any more victims and generally helping to sort out the following day's news bulletin.

Watson took the two men into his office, the aftershave even more pungent than they remembered. 'You will, of course,' said Watson, 'have our full co-operation on this investigation. Anything in particular you'd like access to?'

'At some stage we'll need to see his computer profile. One of the techies will come to have a look at it. At the same time our man can check Felicity's. There might just be something that links the attack on Gordon Bailey with Ms Strutt's disappearance. In the meantime, we'd like to look back at some of the stories Bailey wrote. When did he join you?'

'About nine months ago. Not long before I came here.'

'So he must have reported on a few juicy tales in that time?'

'He often has the lead story. He regularly breaks stories before the opposition. Mind you, there's not much opposition these days. Still, he was good at his job and had a style all his own when he was reporting.'

Davies remained silent, waiting for Watson to continue.

'Gordon covered a few court cases for us. Do you think one of the criminals he reported on could have wanted revenge?'

'I doubt it. I've never come across it before. In fact from what I've heard criminals see it as a badge of honour when reporters cover their trial. If they're sent down they actually brag about the coverage their case gets.

'If a judge says they've committed a heinous crime and they've seen nothing like it in all their years on the bench, that gives the criminal a bit of kudos in jail – earns him respect, ensures that no one else is keen on tackling him. But we'll go through Bailey's reports and see if anything looks odd.'

'How would you like them: hard copies or would you like to see how they appeared on the screen?'

35

At one time the Queen's Medical Centre was the largest hospital in the UK and the biggest teaching hospital in Europe. Despite its size its 1,300 beds were full most of the time and demand increased as the weather deteriorated towards the end of each year.

Davies could just about remember the days when hospitals smelled of a mixture of carbolic soap and stewed cabbage. Queen's was nothing like that; even so, Davies still didn't like going there.

He was always astounded by how busy the hospital was. Everywhere he looked people were scurrying around, either determined to get to an appointment, late because they'd had trouble parking or were bemused by the size of the building.

The only place where people were relaxing was a coffee shop, rented out to a chain which encouraged customers to gorge themselves on cakes and other sweet treats. Ironic, Davies thought, that it was selling the very things that contributed to people requiring treatment on the National Health Service.

Davies made his way to the west block and its familiar C floor. He'd lost count of the number of times he'd visited the intensive care unit to check on the condition of both victims and criminals. He reported to the duty sister who showed him where to wait.

A doctor with the tired eyes of a man who'd put in a long shift took a cursory look at Davies' warrant card. The medic let out a deep sigh. 'I'm so sorry to have to tell you this, inspector – Gordon Bailey died ten minutes ago.'

The incident room was already beginning to look untidy as documents lay on desks waiting to be filed – paperwork was always the last thing to be dealt with when a detailed inquiry was under way. Interviewing potential witnesses, following up forensic reports and sifting through endless hours of CCTV footage always took priority.

Davies spoke as though every second were vital.

'Okay, Gordon Bailey has died in hospital. We're now looking at a second murder investigation. Mark, please bring us up to date.'

Roberts opened a folder in front of him.

'The post-mortem's due later, boss. It looks as though he was beaten to death in the same way as Kevin Michaels. But there's an interesting aspect to this case: one of Gordon Bailey's eyes was gouged out – we're not sure whether that was done before the attack or afterwards.

'We're getting CCTV from Waverley Street and Arboretum Street. Should be a few private houses there with footage.

'As for Kevin Michaels, we've drawn a blank on buses and taxis, so we still need to find out whether anyone picked him up after he left the pub.'

'Thanks, Mark. Let's find out who had a grudge against Gordon Bailey. Why take out one of his eyes? Was someone trying to send a message that he'd seen too much?'

'Boss, it could be a Biblical reference.' The voice belonged to Matt Reynolds, a member of the Christian Police Association.

'There's a verse in Matthew's gospel chapter five. It's all about lust. It says "everyone who looks at a woman with lustful intent has already committed adultery with her in his heart. If your right eye causes you to sin, tear it out and throw it away. For it is better that you lose one of your members than that your whole body be thrown into hell."'

'Bailey could have been having an affair with someone else's wife. Or maybe we're looking for someone who's mentally unstable, who's a religious fanatic.'

Davies thought about the religious material that had been left on the bench at Heage Lane Bridge but pushed it to the back of his mind.

'Thanks, Matt. Whatever the motive, we need to find out if one person killed both Bailey and Kevin Michaels. We've got two reporters who've been brutally murdered – but why? What had they done to deserve being executed in such a callous fashion?'

160

36

As Tilly headed off to the television station to look at some of Gordon Bailey's reports, she imagined what she might find: staff rushing around, tablet computer in their hands, trying to look important and making out they were the only possible person who could do that job.

The scene which greeted her eyes was totally different and not just because fewer people were in on a Sunday. She found everyone was working at a slow pace and there was an aura of death hanging in the air; Gordon Bailey's murder had had a stupefying effect.

She was shown into a small, east-facing room with blinds drawn to blot out the morning sun. There was a chair which looked in no way comfortable, a desk that appeared to have been bought at a very cheap auction and a PC. Tilly was given a crash course in how to bring up Gordon Bailey's stories and was left on her own.

Bailey's face appeared on the monitor, an air of professional competence compensating for his almost scruffy, careworn appearance. A speaker at one end of the desk burst into life as Bailey presented a report about an inquest into the death of a soldier:

'It wasn't the shots from the enemy that killed him – it was shots from his own regiment. His life cruelly, tragically and prematurely ended in a senseless, macho drinking game.'

Tilly understood what everyone said about Bailey having his own individual style.

Another report lit up the screen, this time featuring a hit man who'd pocketed a huge amount of money for killing two targets before police had a slice of luck in arresting him.

'The judge told the defendant these were shocking murders by any standard. But let's put it in layman's terms: he blew away two victims in an appallingly sadistic manner. They might have been low life – but even they shouldn't have been made to suffer so much agony and terror.'

The third report, from a couple of months previously, was the one which really attracted Tilly's interest. Bailey was standing outside a care home in which several people, including disabled men in their twenties, had died. His words were typically acerbic:

'I can exclusively reveal that the company which owns Eureka House behind me and other care homes is being investigated by the police. A major team's looking at incidents going back two years at all the company's homes. One woman's been arrested on suspicion of fraud and neglect – she's been released on bail. I also understand Derbyshire county council has stopped sending residents to Eureka House, and disabled young adults are being removed because of concerns about their safety.'

Tilly pondered what the report had done to the company's credibility and financial position. Had someone decided to get revenge on Bailey? Had he crossed the line and paid the ultimate price? She asked for a copy of Bailey's report to present to DI Davies.

37

Sunday was the day Miles Davies had been looking forward to ever since Lorraine's telephone call. He was up early, managed a five-mile run without doing himself any major harm, showered and had breakfast, all by 9am.

Lorraine arrived shortly afterwards with Jordan and they spent a pleasurable few minutes talking and fussing over their son who enjoyed being the centre of attention.

For the whole time Davies had a smile on his face – so different from the days characterised by fights, sniping and betrayal when Lorraine refused to put up with the time-consuming, relationship-testing nature of Miles' job.

They parted on good terms after Miles had insisted that nothing would prevent him spending the whole day with Jordan nor dropping him off at school the following morning.

Father and son kicked a football around the local park, Jordan showed his dad how good he was at riding his bike and when a shower forced them inside the youngster proved he had more concentration than his dad when finding matching pairs in a card game.

'Okay, Jordan. Where do you want to have lunch?'

'Pizza Hut, please!'

'If that's what you want, that's where we'll go.'

'Great. Mummy only lets me go there when it's my birthday.'

'Well, I won't tell her about it if you don't. Let's keep it a secret between ourselves, shall we?'

Jordan tucked into his Hawaiian pizza and fries, ice cream and a Coke while Davies opted for a pizza with mozzarella, spinach and goat's cheese.

'Looking forward to the game, Jordan?'

'Yes. I've never seen a proper one before.'

'You'll love it. But you've got to watch carefully. It's really fast. You can easily lose track of who's winning.'

'Oh, I won't do that,' said Jordan with the assurance of a boy several years older than himself. 'I've seen games on TV. I'll just look at the scoreboard.'

And you might be a bit disappointed by what you see, thought Davies who was always amazed that Americans could cram so much detail on their scoreboards while the ones in England were much more basic.

The arena began to fill up early for the clash against Leicester Riders, with the visitors bringing a good number of fans. There was an intense rivalry between the two clubs yet it was usually good-natured;

supporters mixed together and there was plenty of mickey-taking. But the banter never escalated into the violence associated with some sports. That was why Davies and many other parents never had reservations about taking their children to basketball, no matter how young they were.

The atmosphere was electric by the time the two teams appeared for the official introductions. Miles and Jordan booed as each of the Riders took to the court. Then the Alan Parsons Project's *Sirius* blasted out of the speakers. Hearts began to beat more quickly. Fans cheered and whooped as the Storm appeared.

Davies quickly finished reading an article in the programme which spelled out the dangers of Leicester Riders as 'a team who like to play uptempo basketball and leave opponents breathless'.

Just before tip-off Tilly slipped into the seat next to Davies. She looked even more ravishing than usual in a short, multi-coloured jacket over a snug-fitting top and expensive-looking jeans. The cool wind had brought colour to her cheeks, giving her a healthy glow. Her make-up was subtle; her eyes sparkled despite the arena's harsh lighting.

Davies smiled again: 'Thought you weren't going to make it.'

'I've discovered a few interesting things about Gordon Bailey. I'll tell you about them later. I've been at the TV station since first thing this morning, so I thought I'd write everything up after the game.

'It's always good to beat Leicester. Who cares if it's a terrible game as long as we win?'

She turned her attention to the boy sitting the other side of Davies. 'You must be Jordan. Hi, I'm Tilly. You okay?'

'Yes, thanks.' The excitement of the game gripped him by the throat and almost prevented him from speaking.

'What do you reckon – have we got a chance?' Davies asked him. He shrugged.

'Tilly?'

'Depends. If we can stop their fast break we should do okay. I don't think they've lost yet this season. I saw them last year and I hate to say it – they were really good. Their coach has recruited a couple of new guys. Supposed to be even better. Storm will have to play flat out for forty minutes to beat them.'

Davies moved closer. 'You sound as though you could be a good candidate if there's a coaching vacancy. Equality and all that – they might go for a female coach.'

'No way. Too much pressure. I did it in one of the local leagues for a year and that was enough. Everybody expected miracles but I just wanted to have a bit of fun. I'll stick to playing the odd game with a few friends down at the leisure centre.'

Riders were quick off the mark and coach Ross had to call an early time-out to try to disrupt Leicester's momentum.

As the team were being given new instructions, Davies looked across at the two Americans in the Storm's line-up. Parker was staring intently at the coach and taking in everything he said while Eliot seemed detached. Was that an air of self-importance, smugness even?

167

Could one or both the Americans have been involved in Michaels' murder? They hadn't been in the country long but they'd had enough time to meet Michaels, fall out with him and take revenge. Yet there was nothing to link them to Gordon Bailey. Maybe they did away with Michaels and Bailey's death was a copycat killing by someone trying to put the police off the scent.

Davies could see Eliot being a troublemaker if he fell in with the wrong crowd. But Parker? Not on the face of it. Perhaps there was something in his make-up that made him turn nasty when provoked. Yet opposing basketball players had tried to goad him without success. Was there something enigmatic about him?

'Daddy, when are they going to start playing again?'

Davies' attention returned to the game. 'Any minute, son. The coach is just trying to get his team to play better.'

The result was instantaneous, although perhaps not as coach Ross intended. Riders' point guard, crouching determinedly as he dribbled the ball up the court, thought he could get the better of his opposite number only for Parker to show astonishingly quick reactions. He stole the ball and set off towards the Riders' hoop.

The Leicester man hared back trying to take up a defensive position, but Parker was aware of a teal uniform streaking past him and lobbed the ball above the rim of the basket. Eliot caught the ball and slammed it through the hoop in one movement.

The crowd were on their feet. Chants of 'Derby! Derby!' reverberated around the arena as it was the Leicester coach's turn to take a time-out.

When play resumed the Riders beefed up their defensive intensity. They stole the ball a few times and played to their main strength: the fast break. Leicester went on a twelve-two run and the Storm had no answer.

Derby reduced the deficit in the fourth quarter but the closest they got was six points before Leicester reasserted their authority and made victory secure.

'Did you enjoy that?' Tilly smiled at Jordan.

'It was amazing!'

'And what was the best part of it?'

'When the big man caught the ball and dunked it in one go. Awesome!'

'I see your dad's taught you the language already.'

Davies stood up and his son did likewise.

'Right, let's go and get you a drink.'

The three of them analysed the game before Tilly went back to work. Davies took a very tired Jordan home, tucked him up in bed and read him a story. Davies was just about to go downstairs when the boy stopped him in his tracks.

'Daddy, is Tilly your girlfriend?'

38

'We've got the details of the company who own the care home that Bailey criticised in his report. We're checking the directors' backgrounds and seeing if any of them have a criminal record. Good job, everybody.

'Next, Felicity Strutt. Anything for us, Paul?'

Allen took the floor: 'Her car. Report from forensics. Her DNA's all over it, of course. And a couple of other people's as well.'

'I presume one of them will be her husband. Tilly, get in touch with Woodcock again. Tell him we've found her car and we want a DNA sample from him. And see if he's got any idea who the third person might be who's been in her car.'

Allen continued: 'We've got the report on her laptop. Nothing incriminating, I'm afraid.'

'Nothing?'

'Not a single word out of place. She didn't slag off her employers, there's no hint of an affair – she didn't even snipe at any of the trolls who occasionally had a go at her on Twitter.'

'What about CCTV?'

'Uniform checked that hotel off Mansfield Road. Remember it? It used to be owned by one of the big chains until recently – they sold it off because it wasn't making enough money. It's been taken over by a private firm.

'They haven't got round to updating their CCTV system yet. They've got a few really old cameras – you struggle to get a reasonable picture from them.'

Allen paused, relishing the fact that everyone in the room was waiting for him to disclose what else he knew.

'We've managed to get a picture of Felicity. There's no doubt it's her. You can tell by her clothing. By the way, does anyone know how tall she is?'

Several of his colleagues groaned. Allen was known as someone who liked to keep his colleagues in suspense, talking in a roundabout way before a major revelation.

Davies was exasperated. 'She's about five foot seven. What's the significance?'

'Well, this was taken on the evening she disappeared, and this is no tall story – the man she's with is about a foot bigger than she is.'

Detective Superintendent Holland summoned Davies into his office. Holland was sipping coffee as though he were in a five-star, internationally respected hotel. He didn't offer Davies a cup, nor did he ask him to sit down.

'Now, Miles, you've got two murders on your hands. How are you getting on with them?'

'There's a lot of evidence to sift through. It might seem a bit slow but we're getting there.'

'Have you come up with a motive for Kevin Michaels' death? Or Gordon Bailey's?'

'We've got a few avenues that we're checking out.'

It was the sort of response Holland heard all the time. He'd trotted it out enough times himself when he didn't want the press to know that an investigation was going nowhere.

'Really. It looks to me as though the only link you've established was that there was a storm on the night that both men were killed.

'And what about Felicity Strutt – what's the latest on her disappearance?'

'You know that's proving difficult. There's still nothing to indicate that she's come to any harm. For all we know she could have decided to make a new life somewhere else. Perhaps she's left her husband and gone off with another man.' The lines on Holland's face multiplied as he gave Davies his sternest look.

'I don't know whether you've been following social media recently but ever since that press conference we've been getting a lot of flak – the consensus is that we don't know what we're doing. We've not had a particularly good relationship with the public over the last few years and we've certainly gone down in their estimation since Felicity vanished.'

Holland put his fingers together and tried to give the impression of being deep in thought. Davies was waiting for the prepared speech he knew was coming. Holland would have said it even if Davies had announced he'd arrested a double murderer and Felicity Strutt had turned up.

'Miles, I must say I'm really disappointed in the way things are going. I thought I could trust you to get the most out of your team but it seems you can't motivate them to get results.'

'I've got the greatest respect for my officers. They don't need motivating – they're loyal, extremely hard-working and they carry out investigations by the book. It's taking longer because we're short of . . .'

Holland held up his hand to silence Davies. He expected Davies to take a reprimand without answering back.

'Look, Miles, I think you need some help.'

'That'll be good. A few more officers will take some of the weight off. There's so much legwork to do.'

'I've told you before – there's no way you can have any more people on your team. Apart from one. I think it's time to call in an expert. One who specialises in offender profiling.'

Davies' head dropped. It wasn't what he was expecting.

'You know my views on profilers. They can lead you down the wrong path. They have too narrow a focus. I'd prefer to keep an open mind about who the killer is.'

'Well I think they can help an investigation that's stalling. And I've got just the man to do that.'

'I suppose he's a good mate of yours.'

'He is, but that's a secondary consideration. He's an associate professor in forensic psychology. If anyone can solve these murders, he can.'

James West rapped on Holland's door and didn't wait to be invited in.

'Boss, there's a man who's asking to see you. Reckons he's the guy who met Felicity on the night she disappeared.'

Before Holland could object, the pair of them dashed out of the office towards the room where Richard Turner was waiting.

He was normally a confident, outgoing character who coped well with whatever life threw at him. Orphaned at an early age, he'd been through broken relationships, redundancy and a cancer scare by the time he was in his mid-twenties.

But on being taken to a police station interview room, he was having trouble keeping his anxieties in check. His leg twitched uncontrollably and his eyes darted around trying to take in every detail of the room even though there was nothing remarkable about the four walls or the floor. Beads of sweat were visible on his forehead and his podgy hands.

He pulled the lapels of his jacket closer together although his increasing waistline made that difficult. Too much food, he acknowledged, which had led to his putting on a couple of stones in weight over the past six months.

He was dressed well enough for any upmarket restaurant, a blue pin-striped suit, white shirt, striped tie and neat haircut giving him the air of a presentable, respectable member of society.

The strip lighting gave out a bright, consistent glow. Didn't they have spotlights any more that they shone in your face to make you confess? He reprimanded himself for watching too many 1950s' detective films.

He looked again at the camera mounted high in the corner of the room. Were they watching him now? Would they be examining his mannerisms so that they knew how he would react to their interrogation? Calm down, he told himself. You volunteered to come here. You've got nothing to be afraid of, so don't get stressed.

The door opened. Davies and West entered. They sat down opposite him.

'Mr Turner, I'm DI Miles Davies and I'm leading the investigation into Felicity Strutt's disappearance. This is Detective Sergeant James West. Thanks very much for coming in, we really do appreciate it. I'd just like to point out that you're free to leave at any time and you're not under arrest.'

Turner sat upright as Davies continued.

'Now, I understand you met Felicity on the evening she disappeared. Is that correct?'

'That's right.'

'Do you know Felicity well?'

'Yes. We've been friends for ages.'

Davies raised an eyebrow at the reply.

'We went to university together. She studied geography, I did politics and international relations.'

'An interesting choice. Did you do well out of it?'

'First-class honours.'

'And did you intend to get a job doing something similar? These days you never know if people are taking a course just to say they've got a degree to their name.'

'Not me. I've been interested in politics since I was a kid. Politics affects everyone. I suppose some people would say I've got strong views: I can't stand people who don't vote at an election. If they can't be bothered to go out and put a cross on a ballot paper, they shouldn't have the right to complain if they think the council or their MP's wasting their money.'

Davies smiled in agreement.

'And what sort of person is Felicity?'

'Some people like her, some hate her. I like her a lot. She can be a bit detached and she gets obsessed with her work. But we have a lot of fun together – on the odd occasion when we find time to meet up.'

'So, on the evening she went missing, she said she was meeting a business associate. Why didn't she say she was seeing a friend?'

'She always likes to sound important. I've told her she takes herself too seriously and should chill out more, but she doesn't take any notice. Not that it bothers me – I accept her as she is.'

Turner revealed that he was a researcher for the Conservative MP Roger Stone. Turner had seen an email from his boss to a lobbying company in which he suggested he would act as a consultant for a considerable amount of money. In return the politician would table amendments to legislation.

When Turner approached his boss about a possible conflict of interest, the MP brushed aside his concerns.

It had the potential to become a huge scandal and Turner decided to let Felicity Strutt know about it.

'Why involve Felicity and not an experienced political reporter? You must know a few,' said Davies.

'Because I thought it could be her big break. She's wasted doing the weather – and she knows it. I reckon she could be a good investigative reporter and if she could pull off this story, the sky would be the limit.'

After a couple of seconds he realised the unintentional pun. 'Or one of the other national TV channels for that matter.'

Davies ignored Turner's nervous laugh.

'That's all well and good, but what about loyalty to your employer – didn't you think about that before you decided to betray him?'

Turner batted the question away with the aplomb of a politician who'd been briefed about answering difficult questions.

'Of course I did. He's shown no loyalty to me. I want to become an MP and I tried to get onto the Conservative Party's

177

approved list of parliamentary candidates. But he wouldn't support me. He blocked my application and refused to say why. So if he won't back me, I've no qualms about telling the world about some of the dodgy practices he gets up to.'

Davies promised he would get one of his colleagues to investigate whether the MP had committed an offence before returning to Turner's meeting with Felicity.

'How long did you spend with her that evening?'

'She picked me up as soon as she'd finished work, not long after seven. We had a meal at a restaurant in town, a couple of drinks – it was a real laugh. The time flew by. It must have been after ten when we left the restaurant.'

Davies assumed it was Turner's DNA that had been found in Felicity's car.

'What sort of a mood was she in? How did she seem?'

'She was fine. She was really looking forward to getting her teeth into the story I'd given her.'

'Did she say where she was going when she left you?'

'I presumed she was going straight home.'

'What about her husband – do they get on?'

'On the face of it. But she confides in me more than anyone else. She told me Rob was getting on her nerves, always wanting to know where she was, always checking up on her. I don't think their marriage will last much longer.'

Davies paused. What if Woodcock had somehow found out that Felicity was leaving him?

'So, if you're close to her, did she take you into her confidence on any other matters? Did she let on that she was having an affair?'

'No, she didn't. I think I'd be the first to know if she was.'

'Were you having an affair with her?'

Turner laughed. 'I love Felicity in a certain way but not like that. Let's just say she couldn't satisfy me in a physical sense.'

West finally broke his silence.

'Okay, what have you done with her?'

'What?'

'You were the last person to be seen with her – the trail ends with you. You've abducted her, haven't you?'

Turner's mouth went dry and his heart started beating much more rapidly. But he looked straight at West: 'She was fine when I last saw her. I don't know where she is but I wouldn't do anything to harm her.'

West stared at Turner. Seconds later Davies pulled out a photograph and placed it in front of Turner.

'Just one last thing. This is a photo of Felicity taken later that evening after you'd left her. Do you know the man she's with?'

Turner looked closely but could only make out the man's height, not his features.

'Big bloke. But I don't think I've ever seen Felicity with him before. Sorry.'

'Thanks very much, Mr Turner. You've been very helpful.' Davies started to show him out.

'Is that it?'

'Yes. We appreciate you coming in. If you think of anything else, you'll let us know, won't you? That's all for now.'

Davies asked Turner to make a formal statement and West led him back to reception.

West returned, looking downcast. 'What was that about, boss? I thought Turner was ready to crack.'

'He's done nothing. Just because he's involved in politics, it doesn't automatically mean he's a liar.'

'Yeah, but I thought he was being a bit secretive.'

'Did you get a good look at him, a really good look? Did you notice he maintained eye contact throughout the interview? He also became quite emotional, especially when he was talking about Felicity. He's like one of those actors in that film, what was it, *The Full Monty*.'

'Eh?'

'Nothing to hide. Pity we can't say the same about Felicity.'

39

Davies managed to find a space on Gill Street, parked his car and headed up Waverley Street past the university's school of art and design and into the Arboretum.

He wandered past the lake where ducks were somersaulting as they showed off in a bid to attract a mate. He came to a bench near the bandstand, one of several listed structures in the park which had been transported there from Nottingham castle more than a hundred and thirty years previously.

A couple of pigeons waddled in front of him as if they had all the time in the world. A squirrel showed more urgency as it skipped across the grass before hurtling out of sight, settling on a branch above head height.

Davies sighed as he read a leaflet which pointed out the various trees with their Latin derivation and their more common names. He felt inadequate when he realised he could recognise so few of the trees. Where was the one that produced foul-smelling fruits that were once eaten by dinosaurs? Had he passed the one that was resistant to atmospheric pollution? And would the one designed to minimise snow damage be able to survive the harsh winter that the weather forecasters were predicting?

It was the same with all the different varieties of plant. His parents had both been keen gardeners but Davies had never shared their enthusiasm for anything horticultural or botanical.

'You must be Miles.' The voice took him by surprise.

'And you must be Jeremy.' They shook hands and sat down on a bench.

Jeremy Hughes was casually dressed but smart, a padded jacket covering an open-necked designer shirt while his trousers had sharp creases and his shoes had been given a good shine that morning. He was in his early fifties yet looked younger, his hair only just beginning to display the odd trace of grey.

'Lovely spot. Nice and quiet,' Davies said.

'I love coming here. Gets you away from the hustle and bustle. Mind you, it's getting a bit cold now. Won't be able to come here for much longer. It can be a bit bleak in the winter.'

Davies was eager to get back to the station but he felt Hughes might just be able to give him the lead he desperately wanted.

'Was it a day like this when Robert Campbell was murdered?'

'It was, actually. Although the weather obviously wasn't the most memorable aspect of the case. Presumably you've read the papers?'

'Yes, I have. You were a detective sergeant at the time, weren't you?'

'That's right. It was just before I was promoted to inspector.'

'I realise you weren't in charge of the case but you're the most senior officer who's still with us.'

'Probably because I got out before it was too late. The force was changing and I couldn't stand how many checks and balances there were. You had to be seen to be doing everything by the book. Too much paperwork. It's much more laid back in private security.'

Davies fidgeted on the hard bench.

'Is there anything that's not in the case files that you can tell me? Not of course that I'm saying you held anything back.' Davies hoped his tone didn't sound accusatory.

'Can't think of anything. Apart from the fact that it left a bit of a bad taste. Because we didn't solve it. That was the annoying thing.'

'Robert Campbell. What sort of a guy was he?'

As Hughes relaxed, his Nottinghamshire accent was discernible. 'From all accounts he was a decent bloke. Very likeable. Would do almost anything for anybody. He was a real community asset. Went to church, practised being a good Christian. Probably the least person you'd expect to be wiped out in the way he was.'

'Do you think he got excited about some of the stuff he was writing? It was something he did on the side, so it might have given him a bit of a thrill and he could have taken things just a bit too far.'

Hughes mulled over the notion. 'It's a possibility. He had a relatively mundane job, so maybe the excitement of seeing his name in print spurred him on to dig out stories that upset someone. He could have got careless and not checked his facts properly. Perhaps someone gave him a story that wasn't a hundred per cent true.'

'And the bottle of ink poured down his throat?'

'We never did get to the bottom of that.'

'But you must have a theory.'

'Just a guess – he could have written something that touched a nerve or he was planning to publish an article that someone didn't want to come out. But it was all speculation.'

Davies' mind was in a whirl. He appreciated what Hughes had told him – but he was no nearer the truth.

'One of my team's got this theory that someone hired a hit man to knock off Campbell and send a message that he'd crossed a line by printing a particular story. The guy who brought in the hit man has now decided to do his own dirty work and take revenge on other journalists who've offended him. What are your thoughts on that?'

Hughes looked up at the sky. Grey clouds were beginning to overpower the landscape.

'I don't think I buy that. Remember all those years ago guns were more readily available than they are now. I sincerely doubt that the killer would wait for twenty years before claiming his next victim.

'Usually serial killers get a thrill out of bumping someone off. Once they start, they have to continue. So I reckon the bloke who murdered Robert Campbell and the man you're looking for are two completely different people.'

40

The television newsroom emitted an aura of shock, grief and loss. Death was something the staff reported on; they didn't usually have to go through the pain and despair of losing one of their team. Naturally staff had lost relatives and close friends, some in tragic circumstances. And those with long memories could recall a long-serving stalwart suffering a fatal heart attack. But that was a one-off.

They weren't just a team – although it sounded contrived, they were like a family. But now one of them was lying in a mortuary and another had vanished.

A few days ago the staff ignored visible faults in their surroundings as they got on with the most important job they faced: putting out a daily half-hour news programme. Now they noticed the areas that were in desperate need of a coat of paint; chairs that had come unstitched and had foam protruding from them; desks that wouldn't even fetch a reasonable price in a second-hand shop.

After each programme there was a meeting which was usually little more than a pat-each-other-on-the-back review, with praise heaped on those who did well and a mild rebuff if anything had gone slightly wrong. That was until the evening Chris Watson gave his critique.

He looked even less suited to the station manager's job than usual, a couple of days without a shave and nights with disturbed sleep giving him a haggard look. A creased shirt and faded jeans added to his unkempt appearance.

A couple of minutes after the half-hour broadcast finished, the staff gathered around for the de-briefing.

'Well, I must say that was one of the worst programmes I've seen for a long time.'

A few of the team who usually didn't pay much attention looked at him with more than mild surprise. Others who were under the impression that everything seemed fine when the programme left the gallery looked at one another quizzically, wondering whether there'd been some technical problem they weren't aware of.

'I'm sick and tired of us doing stories that give councils – and MPs for that matter – a platform to air their views. It's about time we held politicians to account instead of going along with their news agenda. Let's make them sweat a bit more!

'And what's all this with giving airtime to shows that aren't on our network? There's no need for us to be telling people to watch something on another channel. I don't care how popular that programme is.

'Which leads me to another point. We've become too celebrity-focused. Why are we doing pieces about so-called stars who are famous just because they've been caught on camera having a strop about another Z-list celebrity no one's heard of?

'Do you know what the best part of tonight's programme was? The weather. Thank you, Charlotte, for standing in for Felicity. I'm really grateful.

'As for the rest of you, get off your arses and find some decent news stories. I expect much better tomorrow.'

He walked out of the newsroom, everyone wondering whether Watson would turn back to tell them all it was a joke. But he carried on and left the building.

It was a full thirty seconds before mouths closed again and someone spoke.

'What was all that about?'

'Bloody hell,' said the producer. 'I know the programme wasn't the best we've ever put out but I didn't think it was that bad.'

'I suppose he's having a hard time at the moment, what with Gordon's murder and no word on Felicity,' chipped in a correspondent.

The PA who always saw the best in everyone added: 'It can't be easy for him, having to get in touch with Gordon's family. I bet he'll have a lot of the arrangements to make for a memorial for Gordon as well. I do feel sorry for him.'

'What he ought to remember,' said the producer, 'is that we've all been affected in some way by what's happened. We're doing our best. There was really no need for that outburst from Chris. I'm just glad I'm not doing the programme tomorrow.'

41

Davies called everyone to order. 'Sorry we're a bit late getting under way but we've got a few new lines to go at. Mark, bring us up to date.'

Roberts passed around duplicated papers about the Gordon Bailey investigation.

'On the night he was murdered, Bailey was seen in the city centre making a nuisance of himself. A couple of people said he'd had too much to drink. Unsteady on his feet. Not too many people around at the time – just a few dashing around as fast as they could because it was raining so hard.

'We've got a witness who was trying to shelter from the rain. Says she saw Bailey having an argument with a man. Not much of a description. But what she did say was that this man was really tall, much taller than Bailey.

'We've also got another burnt out car. On some waste ground – a couple of miles from the Arboretum. Again, doubtful we'll get DNA off it.'

Davies thanked him before moving on to Felicity Strutt.

'James and I have interviewed an old friend of hers, Richard Turner. He was with her until after ten o'clock on the night she disappeared.'

He looked at the CCTV photograph of Felicity going into the hotel on Mansfield Road. 'This was taken at 10.30pm. We need to know whether this man and the one who was seen with Gordon Bailey are one and the same.

'Anything from the hotel?'

Roberts jumped in. 'We've been up there and although the staff have confirmed it's Felicity, they either can't or won't say who the man is. They weren't keen to tell us much about him, but they did say he'd been spotted there a couple of times before.'

Davies issued a new order: 'I also want one of you to find out as much as you can about the MP Roger Stone and his researcher, Richard Turner who we spoke to earlier.'

'Are they suspects?' a voice at the back chimed up.

'Not necessarily. Turner and Felicity go back a long way. Turner reckons Stone was involved in some dodgy financial deals and Felicity wanted to find out more about them. So let's see where that leads us.

'We're still looking for anything to link Felicity's disappearance and Gordon Bailey's murder. I want someone over at the TV station again to find out whether Bailey did any stories knocking Stone. It wouldn't be the first time that a politician's taken revenge on someone who might have harmed his career.

'That's one for you, Paul – I don't think you'll find much to laugh at in Bailey's reports.'

42

Davies went through his record collection, choosing the Pink Floyd album *Meddle* and going straight to his favourite track *Echoes*. Richard Wright's piercing, experimental grand piano sound at the beginning gave way to Dave Gilmour's familiar guitar licks before Nick Mason's drums came crashing in and Roger Waters' bass pulled everything together.

The remains of a Chinese takeaway consisting of sweet and sour chicken, boiled rice and a spring roll sat in the kitchen, yet another reminder of a long day working on two major inquiries without proper breaks for meals.

His phone rang. Lorraine. He reached for the controls and paused the music.

After their usual tentative greeting, Davies asked if Jordan was okay.

'Yes, he's fine. I just want to thank you for having him at the weekend. He said he had a great time.'

There was a slight pause. Lorraine took a deep breath.

'It's good for him to spend time with his dad. He needs a father's influence, especially at his age.'

'No trouble. I enjoyed having him. Allowed me to forget about work for a while.'

'And how is work?'

'As relentless as ever. Got a couple of difficult cases on the go at the moment. It was good to do a few . . . normal things. And of course to spend time with Jordan.'

Lorraine's voice was soft, comforting even.

'He speaks about you all the time. He's always asking when he's going to see daddy again.'

Davies gulped. He was quick to change the subject.

'How's *your* dad? Did he enjoy the surprise party?'

'Yeah. You know what he's like – says he doesn't want to be the centre of attention but he loves it really. There was a tear in his eye when the lights came on and he saw everyone.'

Davies hesitated before he dared to ask the next question. This was so much tougher than interrogating a suspect in a major investigation.

'And how does your dad get on with your boyfriend?'

'He didn't go. I went on my own.'

'Not had a row, have you?'

'We've split up.' There was a hint of resignation rather than sorrow in her voice.

'Jordan just didn't get on with him. The poor boy. He's been getting a bit disobedient lately, and if Dave told him what to do he'd just shout "you're not my dad" and run up to his room. Dave and I decided the best thing to do was not to see each other any more. For Jordan's sake. Since we separated Jordan's behaviour has improved, thank God.'

She wished she had software on her phone that allowed a video chat; she was desperate to see the reaction on Davies' face.

'Maybe when you've got your next weekend off we could go out together, the three of us. Jordan would love that.'

Tilly relished the chance to get her teeth into a new inquiry, especially as it involved basketball. She was grateful to Davies for getting her to discover if there was anything suspicious about either of the two Storm players, Eliot or Parker. If there was, she was sure she'd find it.

She started by checking out the Derby Storm website. There was nothing to surprise her: anyone with a modicum of knowledge of the game knew that three foreign players were allowed on each team in the British Basketball League. They were usually taken by Americans. The Storm had filled their spots with Eliot and Parker, recommended by the club's network of contacts on the other side of the Atlantic, and a young Bosnian who was regarded as an outstanding prospect.

There wasn't a great deal of information about the Americans apart from where they grew up and which college they went to.

She already knew Eliot had been to Duke. Parker, a native of Missouri, had been to a Christian high school before continuing his education at a Baptist college in Lincoln, Nebraska.

She looked up the Duke website which still listed information about the previous year's team. It confirmed that Eliot was 6ft 10ins tall and weighed 225lbs. He was an 'athletic centre' who gave the team 'much-needed size in the front court'. He had terrific ability and 'ran the floor well'. In his junior year he was second on the team in rebounding and second in the conference for blocking shots. She thought it was a pity he didn't always show that talent while playing for Derby.

In his senior year at Duke, Eliot had started well but halfway through he disappeared from the line-up and didn't play in the post-season tournament.

But what happened from when he stopped playing on the college team until he turned up in Derby?

Tilly then turned to Parker and his sporting prowess. He was recruited by the Baptist college's new head coach Kelvin Stewart. The organisation had given him the job because he would help 'to continue to honor Christ through excellence in athletics'.

Parker's statistics were good but the college didn't play at a particularly high standard; it wasn't enough to earn him a decent job in the States or Europe, so there was really no surprise that he'd come to Derby.

For the fourth time Tilly checked she'd got the correct international code, the right number for the area and for the college campus.

A couple of Tilly's colleagues were manning the night shift and two cleaners were trying to find the tops of desks which had disappeared under a mountain of paperwork.

Tilly tapped in the numbers. Even though she'd made scores of international calls, for some reason she felt nervous about speaking to people who had far more knowledge of basketball than she did.

Seconds later a voice told her she was connected to the switchboard of the Baptist college in Lincoln, Nebraska. She asked to be put through to coach Stewart. She fidgeted and scratched the back of her head as she waited.

'Good afternoon. Kelvin Stewart.'

The voice was quiet but confident. The tone put Tilly at ease. She explained she was a police officer from the East Midlands force in the UK and was making enquiries into a murder.

'During our investigation one young man's name has been mentioned: Rick Parker.'

She paused to let her words sink in.

'You say you're investigating a murder and Rick's been implicated? I can't believe it.'

'I only said his name had cropped up. What sort of person is he?'

Even several thousand miles away Stewart's voice had an air of honesty and reliability.

'Rick was not only one of the best basketball players I've ever had the privilege of coaching, he was also one of the finest people I've come across. He's a good, Christian boy; he loves his family, goes to church regularly and will no doubt be a fine, upstanding member of any community that he lives in. He was a good role model here and I had no hesitation in making him the team captain. I just can't believe he'd be involved in any criminal activity. Can you tell me a little about the circumstances?'

'I'm afraid I'm not at liberty to divulge anything. All I can say is a reporter who covered basketball games in England has been found dead. May I ask: have you heard of anyone by the name of Yandel Eliot?'

The line went quiet. It was several seconds before Stewart answered.

'Is that the Yandel Eliot who played at Duke?'

'That's right.'

'I do know of him, yes.'

'He's now playing on the same team in England as Rick Parker.'

'Really. And do they get on?'

'I believe they do. We think Eliot is involved in something that may not be above board. Parker could be covering up for him. What can you tell me about Eliot?'

'There were rumours but nothing was proven.'

'And those rumours were . . . ?'

'It's not my place to repeat gossip. You'll have to speak to someone with a more in-depth knowledge of Mr Eliot than myself.'

43

Staff at the television centre were used to strange people going into their building and disrupting their work. But it didn't make them feel any safer. Fear was evident everywhere as even those with the most menial job contemplated whether they would be the killer's next victim.

Anyone on Davies' team could have reassured them that the odds of the killer striking again or another member of staff disappearing were highly unlikely. But when there was a murderer on the loose, people tended to think and act irrationally.

The management made only one demand of the police: that they didn't get in the way when a news bulletin was approaching, and officers were happy to comply.

The interlopers were easy to spot: their visitor's badge was clipped to an outer garment whereas staff had an identity card hanging from a lanyard around their neck. They took little comfort from the fact that protocol was being observed at all times.

After forensics had examined every piece of paper that had been left on a desk by an untidy reporter and every drawer, cupboard and filing cabinet had been taken apart, it was the turn of the IT experts to see what they could discover.

For the second day two computer boffins – one long-haired, the other with his head shaved, both wearing jeans and a T-shirt with an unrecognizable logo – searched through the guts of the office PCs, bringing up on the screens a language that hardly anyone else in the building spoke. One was checking Gordon Bailey's profile, the other who needed no excuse to nip off for a tea or coffee was looking at Felicity Strutt's history.

Between them they went through several thousand emails, the great majority of them not worth even a second look. The average person in the street might have imagined that access to a television personality's emails would lead to a startling revelation; a chance to meet a movie superstar; gossip about a celebrity; a curt reply to a request to interview a government minister. But most of them were about mundane subjects, everything from the arrival of hot food courtesy of a mobile catering van to internal adverts for jobs in an unappealing part of the country which had been sent to staff who didn't have the necessary qualifications for the job anyway.

The IT man looking through Bailey's computer eventually unearthed an email which required more than a cursory glance. It was from Chris Watson. *Legal action* was the bold heading.

Gordon, I've had lawyers for Eureka House going crazy about your story and the allegations you made against the company. They say the story is 'totally untrue and without foundation'. They're threatening legal action unless we issue a retraction and guarantee not to repeat any of the contents of your report.

Where did you get the story from? And are you sure it's kosher?

Bailey had issued a curt reply: *Do you think a journalist with my experience would make up a story like that? Of course it's true. And our lawyers went through every word of it before they allowed it to go on air. Stop being so jumpy!*

The techie copied the email onto a memory stick and went to show his companion who'd been given space at the other end of the office. As he got there his colleague stopped tapping at the keyboard and stared dumbfounded at the screen. In Felicity Strutt's deleted emails box he found one from bridgfordbilly@hotmail.com:

Hi Felicity. I'm one of your biggest fans. I love the way you present the weather forecast. You're my dream woman. I noticed tonight when you were on TV that you were no longer wearing a ring on your left hand. I don't know whether the time is right – you might be going through a few problems in your private life. But is there any chance of a date? I know you must get propositions like this all the time but I'm serious, I really would like to get to know you better. I'm sure we could have some great times together. But please, don't keep me waiting too long . . .

There was no record of Felicity replying to the email. It was dated a week before she disappeared.

44

Thompson turned onto a small path on the estate he knew so well. He noticed that either side there was grass in desperate need of a cut, weeds that ought to have been removed weeks ago and flowers that had neither life nor colour in them.

He rapped four times on the door and waited. Julie Mason eased it open. Her eyes were red from constant crying but she produced a hint of a smile on seeing Thompson.

'Hello, Ken. Do you want to come in?'

Thompson sat in a brown, unfashionable armchair which had been comfortable once, although he realised it must have been a long time ago.

'Julie, I'll come straight to the point. There's a cancer treatment centre in New York. I've been in touch with them and they'll take Ethan.

'You, your daughter and Ethan will need passports. I've brought the forms with me and I'll help you to fill them in. It may take a month or more but you can't get them quicker than that.

'As soon as the passports arrive in the post, let me know and I'll sort out your plane tickets. The flight should be fairly early in the morning, so I'll book you into a hotel near the airport the night before and get Damien to drive you there.

'I'm sorting out an apartment for you while you're in New York. There'll be plenty of money to tide you over. If you're running short, give me a ring and I'll get some more sent out to you. I just want you to bring Ethan home when he's on the road to recovery.'

Tears were again flowing down Julie's cheeks as if someone had turned on a tap.

'I'll never be able to thank you enough. I can't possibly repay all the money for the trip.'

'Don't think about that. Consider it an early birthday present for Ethan. What are friends for if it's not to help each other?'

The road out of Nottingham city centre was busy, even in the early evening after most of the commuters had suffered their second monotonous trip through traffic that day.

Richard Turner gripped his steering wheel and imagined it was how American cops felt when they were tailing a suspect or how Martin Shaw acted when he was in *The Professionals*. Turner had been so impressed after he saw Shaw in a touring version of Reginald Rose's courtroom drama *Twelve Angry Men* that he researched everything Shaw had been in and constantly watched re-runs of the actor playing one half of Bodie and Doyle.

Turner wasn't born the first time *The Professionals* was shown and he would have relished a career in the crime-fighting unit CI5 or some other organisation whose principles were never influenced by the whims of politicians.

Once Turner passed the Queen's Medical Centre and the Priory roundabout he gripped the wheel even more tightly as the A52 opened up into a three-lane carriageway. His determination to find out where Stone was going after cancelling a constituency meeting at short notice meant his common sense had deserted him. Was it really a good idea to try to follow his boss?

Stone was driving a relatively new, fairly powerful gas-guzzler of a car and Turner struggled to keep up in his old, cheap runaround that hardly ever left the city boundary.

Turner's boneshaker rattled and whined as he tried to push it over 80mph. At one point he was ready to turn back as the gap between the two cars grew increasingly wider.

But then a silver-haired man in an ancient Morris Minor decided to overtake a supermarket delivery lorry. He refused to be intimidated as Stone flashed his lights and sounded his horn as he was unable to get past. It allowed Turner to catch up.

Stone eventually accelerated hard again, forcing Turner to break into another cold sweat. But the lights at the Pentagon roundabout, the entrance to Derby's bewildering traffic system, were on red and the relieved researcher was able to pull up only a couple of cars' lengths behind the MP.

From there it was easy for Turner to follow Stone into the city centre where both parked in St Mary's Gate. Stone was relatively close to the Cathedral Quarter Hotel; Turner left his car further up the street but not close enough to be spotted.

Erected in the late 19th century, the hotel had been used as a police station and council offices before being taken over by a private company. It was turned into a swanky boutique hotel – one of the top ten in the country, according to its guests.

It retained many of the original features including a majestic staircase, opulent pillars and an impressive mosaic floor which was almost too good to walk on.

'May I help you?'

An efficient-looking receptionist in a brown uniform and elegantly coiffed hair greeted Turner whose eyes moved from side to side in the unfamiliar surroundings.

His heart palpitated. 'Oh, sorry, I'm here to meet a friend. I've not been here before so I'm not sure where he'll be.' The speech sounded rehearsed because it was.

'Well, he could be in the lounge but it's more likely that he'll be just through there, in the bar.'

Turner took a couple of cautious steps to the left, then turned to see whether the receptionist was still looking in his direction. But she was already moving away to welcome more guests.

Turner saw three men standing just inside the bar. Stone's long, greying hair which was beginning to curl up at the back was unmistakeable. The two others were both dressed in suits and ties; Turner didn't know either of them.

He took out his smartphone, checked that the flash was off, looked around to make sure no one was watching and photographed the trio. He was dying for a brandy – but Stone was bound to recognise him if he went anywhere near the bar.

He turned and in his hurry to get away he bumped into an elegantly dressed couple arriving for dinner. Heart again pounding, he apologised and slinked out of the hotel; he'd had enough excitement for one evening.

45

Tilly took a quick swig of her coffee before making her second call to the United States. She sat back in her chair but almost jumped up when a voice bellowed: 'Coach Andersson.'

She didn't expect to get straight through to Steve Andersson, a former assistant at the renowned and highly successful Duke who'd moved on to a head coach's position at a different college.

'Hello?'

'Yes, ma'am, what do you want?'

Tilly stuttered as she explained she was a detective constable from the East Midlands police force and was calling from Nottingham, England.

'Nottingham. The home of Robin Hood, right?'

She assured him it was.

'And do you meet any people these days who rob the rich and give to the poor?'

'The thieves I come across usually do it purely for selfish reasons.'

'Anyhow, I'm real busy right now,' he barked with a Brooklyn accent. 'I've got practice starting in a few minutes. How can I help you?'

Tilly told him about Kevin Michaels' murder. She mentioned Yandel Eliot's possible involvement.

'What sort of person was he when he played for your team?'

'As a basketball player he could have gone on to play at a high level. Maybe not the NBA but he could have got a spot on a very good European team. But his work ethic was questionable. Sometimes he took his problems onto the basketball court with him.'

Tilly took a deep breath before asking the next question: 'You and Mr Eliot both left Duke at about the same time, didn't you?'

'Purely a coincidence. I was offered a better position, whereas Yandel was not performing to the best of his ability.'

Tilly's knowledge of basketball made her suspicious about Andersson's reply. 'A better position than Duke? Some people might find that hard to believe.'

'And that's what you might think, ma'am. But there was little prospect of advancement at Duke and I'm now a head coach.'

But only at a second or third-rate college, Tilly thought.

'And was it a coincidence that both you and Mr Eliot were investigated over allegations of bribery and fraud?'

'Nothing was proven,' snapped Andersson. 'I denied all wrongdoing at the time and still do.'

Tilly recovered her composure, immediately firing off her next question.

'Some people will say there's no smoke without fire. What do you have to say about that?'

Andersson remained unruffled. 'Corruption is a fact of life in college basketball. There are always people offering incentives to players to join a particular school. Once they sign, they're given presents to show how valuable they are. The players can't get paid, so they're keen to pick up a few fringe benefits. If someone makes it to the NBA, everyone's happy.

'The authorities believe head coaches at major schools don't need to get involved in any dubious activities. Usually they're earning so much money they don't need to risk getting caught up in a corruption case. So it's the assistant coaches who come under scrutiny, and there are quite a few who are prepared to take a chance on not being caught. I was NOT one of them.'

Tilly pondered whether Andersson would be prepared to take a risk. But she knew she had to get him to open up about Eliot.

'Is it true that Yandel didn't play on the team for much of his final year in college?'

'That is correct, detective.'

'Would you like to tell me anything about that?'

'There were certain accusations against him. Drugs were found in the accommodation he shared with a fellow student who was not on the basketball programme. Yandel swore it had nothing to do with him but as the police here were involved we decided to suspend him from the team. At virtually the same time Yandel's girlfriend announced she was pregnant. His head was all over the place. He did not play again for the college and he did not graduate. That was the last I heard of him. I presumed he would become yet another young man who did not live up to his potential as a sportsman or an American citizen.'

'And what happened to his girlfriend?'

'I have no idea. I believe she and Yandel went their separate ways not long afterwards. I have no knowledge of where she is now or if she did in fact give birth.'

Tilly thanked him, put the phone down and started to write her report. She expected that DI Davies would want to speak again to Eliot, this time in an official setting.

46

'Well, my darling, have you had a good day?'

The woman shuddered when she heard her captor's gravelly voice. Her mouth was drier than a desert where no rain had fallen for a month; her head throbbed, affecting her ability to think clearly; she looked embarrassed as her stomach gurgled and groaned.

'I expect you'll be needing a drink.'

He uncapped a small bottle of mineral water and poured some of it down her throat. She swallowed as much as possible before coughing and spluttering as the liquid spilled over her front. She turned her head, the water cooling her neck and breasts while she was regulating her breathing.

He untied one wrist but made sure the other was firmly clamped to the bed.

'Here's your dinner, prepared by my own fair hand. I'm sure it'll come up to your usual standard.'

He placed a tray in her lap. It contained a plate full of fatty food swimming in grease. There was a fork but no knife. She grabbed the fork tightly but the man moved out of stabbing range. She grimaced as she looked at the disgusting mess on the plate but devoured the food anyway – she had no idea when she would eat again.

Richard Turner emptied his pockets, the contents filling up a small coffee table in his one-bedroomed, comfortless flat. After several moments of intense searching he found the business card he was desperate to locate.

He rang the number and had to wait only a couple of seconds before he heard a voice at the other end.

'DI Davies.'

'Hello, inspector. This is Richard Turner, Roger Stone's researcher. Remember me?'

'Yes, of course. What can I do for you?'

'Well, you know I said I thought my boss was involved in something underhand? He called off a pretty important engagement last night so that he could meet a couple of business associates.'

'That's not a crime, Mr Turner. Have you got anything else to go on?'

'I might have. I followed him to a hotel in Derby. He met two guys there. I don't know them but they both looked a bit shady.'

'What do you mean by shady? Can you identify these two men?'

'I can do better than that. I've got a picture of them.'

Half an hour later Davies and Turner met in a coffee shop outside the city centre. Although it was part of a chain, the staff were welcoming, chattering away as they took customers' orders. Turner opted for a white chocolate mocha with whipped cream covered with chocolate powder. Davies settled for an Americano – black with no sugar.

'Mr Turner, what's all this about a picture?'

His podgy hands toyed with his cup before he took a big drink.

'Take a look at this. I managed to get a shot on my smartphone without them noticing. Stone's the one in the middle. I don't know the other two.'

Davies's eyes widened. He moved the phone closer to his face to get a better look.

'Well, any idea who it is?' Turner watched as a stern expression appeared on Davies' face.

'Mr Turner. I'd be grateful if you'd send me this picture. I must ask you not to mention this to anyone else for the time being. Do I make myself clear?'

Turner almost dropped his spoon as he scooped up a dollop of cream.

'I . . . I don't understand. Wh-what's this about?'

'The guy on the right of the picture is Geoffrey Gastrell. Owns a string of care homes. As for the other one, I'm asking for your co-operation until I can find out why he was meeting Stone. He's a detective superintendent in our force. His name's Keith Holland.'

47

Doubled up in pain and gasping for breath, a couple of the Storm players looked ill; they had red faces, sweat was dripping from them and their hearts were pumping faster than they'd ever done before.

Coach Ross expected Yandel Eliot was going to be one of the strugglers; his premonition proved to be correct.

Ross' quiet, measured voice could hardly be heard as he addressed his team.

'Gentlemen, this team is built on speed and athleticism. We may be lacking in height but we can compensate for that with quickness up and down the floor. That means we need to be fitter than our opponents. In case you're wondering, that's why we run so hard at the beginning of each training session.'

Rick Parker, looking as though he'd been out for a gentle, early-morning stroll, took in every word.

'Now, let's go five on five. The starters from the last game will go up against those who came off the bench. Rick, let's try the new offence we introduced against Leicester.'

Parker brought the ball up the court, confidence and control evident with every step.

Eliot moved towards him to set a screen only for his marker to push him out of the way, catching Eliot on the side of his face with his elbow.

'You bastard!' the big man shouted and threw a punch – but his marker had already moved out of the way.

Coach Ross gave a sharp blast on his whistle and was alongside Eliot before he could aim a second blow.

'Calm down, Yandel, you're no good to the team if you're back in the locker room sitting out the rest of the game.'

'No one does that to me, coach. I ain't taking that shit from nobody.'

Ross put his arm around his protégée. 'You must know there are teams in this league that *want* you to lose your composure. They have not got your talent, so they'll try to beat you any way they can. They'll talk trash, they'll tell you your mother was a whore – but you've got to keep cool and rise above it. Make the opposition pay with a few highlight dunks. That will demoralise them more than anything. Now, Rick, run that play again.'

Parker did as he was told. Again Eliot's marker took a physical approach and refused to concede ground only for Eliot to hit him twice before his teammates grabbed hold of him.

Coach Ross' voice maintained its detached tone: 'Yandel, I don't know what's bothering you today but I suggest you shower and change.

You can spend the rest of the session deciding whether you still want to be a part of this team.'

Davies took West to one side and made sure no one was within earshot. 'Okay, let's nip out for a break. There's something I need to run past you.'

Davies bought them both a sandwich and a coffee from the nearest café. They both devoured their food as though they hadn't eaten for days.

'Okay, what's up?' West asked.

A man in a long overcoat sat at the far end of the café, caressing a small cup of coffee as he tried to keep out the cold. A couple of middle-aged women were chattering near the door, oblivious to anyone else in the building. Two other women, younger and with children in the latest and most expensive pushchairs, discussed fashion and beauty treatments.

'Keep this to ourselves. Richard Turner, Roger Stone's researcher, has been checking up on his boss. Saw him meet a couple of people in a hotel in Derby. There's someone new we've got to consider in relation to Gordon Bailey's murder – someone a bit closer to home.'

'Really? I can't think of anyone on our team who would want to get rid of Bailey.'

'It may not be immediately obvious. Cast your mind back to the last press conference we organised. Bailey really had a go at the detective superintendent.'

Davies felt a tinge of guilt that he'd asked Adam Walton to find someone who'd give Holland a hard time.

'Now, if Bailey was on the verge of uncovering something which could implicate Holland, he might have decided things had gone far enough. We've got to look on Holland as a possible suspect.'

48

Jason Ross' office, with its single-pedestal desk and three chairs, was much smaller than he was used to when he coached in the US. But he didn't measure success by the size of the room bearing his name on the door.

The Storm job had come at just the right time for him: his daughter and son were both settled in college and he felt a move to England would improve his CV. Establishing a winning team in Derby could enhance his chances of securing a better position back home or it might lead to a sought-after job in Germany, Spain or Russia.

Ross made the office as cosy as he could: there were photographs of his children as well as one of his wife who was going to join him in a month once she'd finished a job she was tied to.

Inspirational slogans covered the walls and reflected Ross' philosophy. There was one from Phil Jackson who won eleven NBA titles, six with the Chicago Bulls and five with the Los Angeles Lakers: 'Good teams become great ones only when the members trust each other enough to surrender the Me for the We.'

Pat Riley, one of the top ten coaches in NBA history and the first to win a championship as a player, coach and executive, was responsible for 'Excellence is the gradual result of always striving to do better.'

A laptop sat open on the desk, kept fully charged at all times so that Ross could watch footage of potential signings or games featuring the Storm's next opponents.

The late Chuck Daly, coach to the Detroit Pistons when they won the NBA championship in 1989 and 1990, offered: 'To play defense and not foul is an art that must be mastered if you are going to be successful.'

A cautious knock on the door was followed by Ross' unmistakeable yet gentle voice: 'Come in.'

Yandel Eliot ducked as he entered the room and stood in front of the man who would extend or cut short his Storm career.

Eliot, wearing a club sweatshirt, jogging pants and trainers, shifted uncontrollably from foot to foot.

'Sit down, Yandel.'

Eliot grabbed one of the chairs and sat opposite the coach.

Ross wore a suit with a crisp, white shirt and unostentatious tie on game days. Now he wore a button-down casual shirt and chinos.

'Yandel, how are you finding things here?'

'Well, coach, it was a bit difficult at first, moving to a new country and all that, but I think I'm settling in pretty good now. I like Derby. It's a good place to be.'

'I'm delighted to hear it. But what was that little episode in practice all about?'

'I just got a little bit riled, that's all. It won't happen again.'

Ross' voice maintained its composure and calmness. 'I hope it doesn't. I can't afford any of my team sitting out through suspension. At the beginning of the season I gave you an opportunity to resurrect your career here in Derby. I spoke to several people who advised me not to sign you. Said you were too much of a risk. But I saw that you'd been going through a few personal problems. You have good, sound basketball skills. I thought you deserved another chance. Have those problems occurred again?'

Eliot didn't take his eyes off Ross for a second.

'No, sir. That part of my life is behind me. I have no desire to see my ex-girlfriend again. She really messed up my head. She said she didn't want me to have any part in my daughter's upbringing. It hit me really hard at the time but I feel I have to move on. I'm grateful to you, coach, for this opportunity. Coming to a new country has really helped. Now I want to win a championship for the Derby Storm.'

Ross stood up and moved towards the door. Eliot got to his feet, his large frame dominating the room. Ross realised he had to be a father figure and a confidant as well as a coach.

'Good to hear it. But I want you to know that you can always talk to me if anything is bothering you. Doesn't matter what it is. Let's have no secrets from each other, okay?'

Eliot looked at the floor before he turned and walked out of the office.

Daylight had disappeared long before the team reassembled for the early-evening briefing. The enthusiasm which had been apparent at the beginning of the day was waning; energy levels were low.

'Right, let's get this over with. The sooner we're done the quicker we can go home. Or to the pub. Mark, anything to report?'

Roberts was his usual businesslike self, presenting his findings clearly and succinctly.

'Gordon Bailey: starting with his bank account, he's a couple of grand overdrawn. Not unusual for someone who enjoyed drinking with contacts. We're going through CCTV – up to now we've picked him up going to a few places in the city centre and staying there for a good hour or so. Still not sure where he was actually attacked.

'We've made a start on his mobile phone records but there are so many numbers to check. He spent a lot of time on the phone. As a reporter he gave his number out to loads of people that he met. It appears he kept in touch with many of his contacts, so it'll take some time before we can go through everything.

'Social media: it's almost non-existent. Looks as though his bosses encouraged all the staff to post regular updates about the stories they were covering, but Bailey hardly ever did. He was an old-school journalist, so I suppose he didn't buy into the modern concept of connecting with people online.'

Davies expressed his gratitude before consulting his papers even though he knew what the top one contained.

'Alex Wright has just let me have the post-mortem results. You won't be surprised to hear that Bailey died from multiple injuries, just like Michaels. So although Bailey was taken to hospital really quickly, the doctors couldn't do anything to save him.

'Now, let's have a quick look at the Felicity Strutt investigation.'

Paul Allen again addressed the room. 'Boss, this email Felicity received from the guy calling himself Bridgford Billy. Might have chosen the name to put us off the scent.

'The techies have traced the account to a pay-as-you-go mobile phone. Both paid for and topped up with cash. Nothing to link it to the person who set it up. Seems that Billy didn't want anyone finding out who he is.'

49

Davies was mooching. Rain was hammering against the windowpanes, making the dark evening even more depressing. He wasn't in the mood for socialising, so he turned to his record collection to find something to entertain him.

He paused at the letter 'G', the discs being impeccably arranged in alphabetical order. A few albums by Genesis including *Nursery Cryme*. The initial song *The Musical Box* – a gruesome fairy story set in Victorian Britain – was one of his all-time favourites.

He'd played it several times in recent weeks, so he moved on to *We Can't Dance*. Looking at the track list he spotted the fourth number, *Jesus He Knows Me*. He returned the album to its place, turned off his audio system and picked up his phone.

'Jeff, I need to pick your brains, Usual place, fifteen minutes?'

Davies shook his umbrella and threw his raincoat over a wooden chair, a relic of the days when pubs were community hubs that welcomed anyone with a thirst.

He could just about remember his parents giving him a soft drink and a packet of crisps to keep him occupied on their occasional visits to their local.

Nowadays Davies looked forward to dropping in to this establishment which still catered for serious drinkers in need of a satisfying pint.

'Hello, Miles. My shout. What can I get you?'

The first thing that stuck out about Jeff Coxon-Brown was his long, wavy hair which had gone out of fashion decades previously and didn't fit in with his youthful appearance. People noticed his casual clothes next, the Derby Storm sweatshirt and the distressed jeans with holes around the knees. It was only when anyone took a closer look that they realised he was wearing a clerical shirt with a tab collar.

Not the way people expected a man of the cloth to dress. And not the place you'd expect someone in his position to frequent.

But Jeff Coxon-Brown wasn't a conventional vicar. Adopting the catchphrase 'if the mountain won't come to Muhammad, then Muhammad must go to the mountain', he often held services in unconventional places. The pub was one of them.

Those who turned up on a Sunday lunchtime didn't have to sing hymns that were either obscure or so well-known that they'd lost their significance. Coxon-Brown brought in some of his friends who usually played in a rock 'n' roll band. They belted out religious, uptempo songs about how Jesus was in control despite all the suffering and hardship in the world.

They usually had simple but rousing choruses. The 'congregation' found it difficult to resist the temptation to join in.

'How can I help, Miles?'

'You know the Derby Storm players well, don't you?'

'Not amazingly well. Some of them have only been here a few months. A couple have come to me asking for spiritual guidance.

'I've obviously met all the others but I wouldn't say I knew all of them inside out. It comes with the job. I think the Storm are still the only basketball club in the UK with their own chaplain.'

'Don't you find that a bit strange?'

'Not really. I have to go where God tells me. You can find Him on a basketball court as well as in a church. I reckon it's a great gig.'

Davies was surprised to hear Coxon-Brown use that phrase but carried on.

'I'd like your take on something. We're investigating two murders. We haven't got a lot of evidence but there's one thing they've got in common: in each case the prime suspect is someone who's very tall.

'We're checking everyone over a certain height. Naturally enough my boss has pointed out that there could be some basketball players who fit the description.

'So, do you think any of the Storm players could be involved?'

Coxon-Brown almost choked on his non-alcoholic wine.

'Wow, I didn't see that coming!'

He placed his glass back on the table and looked around, trying to hide his discomfort.

'I don't think I'm giving anybody's secrets away when I say that basketball is full of emotion. More so than a lot of sports. Bit of a rollercoaster ride.

'When you're playing two or three games a week, training every day if you're not playing and living in the same house, teammates get to know all about each other. Maybe they know too much.

'Players can get very high when they win and really low when they lose. If they've lost a couple of games and go out for a few beers afterwards, their behaviour can change. We know how alcohol can affect people's judgement and make them lose their inhibitions.'

Davies thought about his evening with Alex Wright and nodded.

'Okay, Jeff, let's look at a couple of players in particular. Yandel Eliot.'

'A complicated character. Sometimes you can speak to him and he's a perfect gentleman. Other times he can't make the effort to engage in conversation.

'Don't know whether he's got mental health problems. That would have to come from someone with medical knowledge. But there are times when things seem to be building up and affecting his stress levels. It could be the responsibility of carrying the basketball team or it could be something totally different.'

Davies realised his glass was empty and wondered whether he dared risk another drink.

'And what about Rick Parker? Seems a level-headed young man. Do you see anything in him that worries you?'

'Rick? Not in the slightest.'

'But if Eliot is having one of those days when he's being a bit – shall we say – carefree, d'you think he might exert pressure on Parker that would send him off the rails?'

Coxon-Brown replied without hesitating: 'No way. Likely to be the other way round. Parker's the steadying influence. I'm sure he'd do everything to keep Eliot out of trouble.

'At times Eliot might look as though he could murder someone on the basketball court. But off it – I can't see it.'

Davies understood Coxon-Brown's thinking. But Parker couldn't be with Eliot 24 hours a day . . .

50

The receptionist at the TV station recognised the two detectives who marched through the double doors and stood in front of her.

She patted her hair to ensure it was in place before greeting the pair. She issued them with their visitors' badges as they signed in.

'Good morning, gentlemen. Here to see Mr Watson again, aren't you?'

Davies fastened the ID badge to the breast pocket of his jacket and Roberts followed suit.

'He's taken the morning meeting, so he should be able to see you now.'

She let them through a security door and returned to her desk. 'You know your way up to his office, don't you?'

Both detectives smiled as they headed towards the stairs.

Chris Watson ushered them into his office and closed the door.

'Is there any news about Felicity?'

Davies thought it strange that Watson wanted to know about his missing weather presenter and made no reference to the fact that one of his staff had been murdered.

'No, not at the moment. We want to talk to you about Gordon Bailey. Where were you on the night he was attacked?'

Watson's eyes darted around the room. 'I can't remember without checking. I'll have to look at my diary.'

While he brought up a list of engagements on his company laptop, Davies noted there were no photographs of Watson's family on his desk or anywhere else in the office. A fountain pen with a gold nib sat in its open box near a smartphone in an expensive-looking leather case.

'Oh, of course, I remember now,' Watson said, his hand covering part of his mouth. 'We had a meeting after the programme about a new series that we're thinking of commissioning. Then I picked up a takeaway on the way home.'

'Can anyone verify that?'

'Inspector, I live alone – apart from my cat. Maybe you'd like to ask him what time I got back?'

West jumped in. 'Well, you must be able to remember which takeaway you stopped off at.'

'Er, I think it was a Chinese on Nuthall Road.'

'And how did you pay for it?'

'With cash. They don't take cards. Why do you ask?'

'Well,' said West, 'if you'd paid for it on a card, the takeaway would have a record of it. So I suppose we'll just have to take your word for it. Unless of course we can get anything out of your cat.'

Watson got to his feet and stood right next to Davies.

228

'Look, what's all this about?'

'It's been brought to our attention that Gordon Bailey got into an argument with someone fitting your description not long before he was killed.'

Watson threw back his head and laughed. 'Inspector, you've got it all wrong. I was nowhere near the city centre.'

'We've only got your word for it. We know you and Bailey weren't on the best of terms. You could quite easily have seen him while he was on one of his pub crawls, had an argument and decided he'd gone too far.'

'That's so untrue it's laughable. Now, if you'll excuse me, I've got a TV station to run.'

51

Holland walked into Davies' office without knocking. 'Miles, this is Leyton Cook. Forensic psychologist. He's got some interesting theories about our murderer. He's come a long way to tell you about them. I'm sure you'll make him welcome.' His smile had a wicked tinge as he left the room.

They shook hands. Davies was surprised to discover the newcomer's limp, moist grip and imagined it was like taking hold of a wet fish. Cook, middle-aged and with a slight paunch, was casually dressed in a loose-fitting jacket, white shirt and blue jeans. His hair, falling over his collar but receding at the front, needed a trim, as did his full beard.

He spoke with confidence and composure.

'Keith tells me you're having problems finding the man responsible for these killings. There are some classic signs you should be looking out for.

'Let's look at a serial killer's motive. Usually you can put it in one of four categories: mission-oriented, hedonistic, control and visionary.

'Unlikely that it's visionary – this is normally when someone believes God or the devil tells them to go out and commit murder.'

Davies suddenly thought about the briefing when Matt Reynolds quoted from the Bible. Could the killer have a warped view that he was doing God's will when he ended Bailey's life?

Cook ploughed on. 'My view is that these murders are mission-oriented and the killer is doing his bit for society by getting rid of the victims. In other cases I've come across, the murderer wants to eliminate gay people or prostitutes, but in this instance it's journalists. I'm sure there are millions of people in this country who can't stand reporters, especially those who've seen their names printed in a newspaper. But there'll only be a small number who will actually go out and kill not just one but two journalists.'

Davies, irritated by the smugness on Cook's face, pretended to be taking in the theory. He clasped his hands and looked into space.

'Interesting observation. But you don't think the motive could include more than one of those categories? Are you trying to tell me the killer isn't exerting some kind of power or control over his victims? And isn't there a hedonistic side to him as well? Doesn't he take pleasure from killing people he regards as expendable?'

Cook dismissed Davies' comments. 'Mark my words: your killer is a man with a mental illness who believes his vocation is to make the world a safer place by killing reporters.

'You should concentrate on someone who lives fairly close to the murder scenes. It will be someone with a low IQ who's got an unskilled job or is unemployed. Look for problems in the home – his parents might be divorced, the influence of a father or mother might be absent. He could also have been abused either sexually or emotionally by a member of his family.'

Davies noticed Cook grow in stature as he continued, convinced he would point Davies in the direction of the killer.

'I'd say our man is definitely a disorganised serial killer. He's impulsive and made no attempt to hide the bodies. From now on, expect him to become over-confident. If he tries to do away with anyone else – and heaven forbid that he does – he's likely to take more risks. That's how you're going to catch him.'

Davies knew he should walk away but the urge to put Cook in his place got the better of him.

'So, what should we do? Put a 24-hour watch on every journalist in the East Midlands?

'You think he's impulsive, eh? So there just happened to be a fountain pen lying around, the killer picked it up and stuck it in Kevin Michaels' chest. Was it the same with Gordon Bailey? Did someone leave a sharp implement lying around and the killer thought it was just what he needed to gouge Bailey's eye out?

'Yes, I know he made no attempt to hide the bodies, but I think the man we're after is pretty organised. He didn't meet Michaels and Bailey purely by chance and decide on a whim to end their lives. He's planned the killings meticulously. The bodies were found twenty miles apart. Sounds like our man knows what he's doing. And I reckon that's beyond someone who's not very brainy.

'The killer had a definite reason for murdering these two journalists. That's the key to solving the case.

'Now I'm going for a coffee. You can read a deeper meaning into that if you want – but for me it means I need a caffeine hit.'

52

West brought Davies a strong coffee and a tea for himself. They were ready to question Yandel Eliot; he'd reluctantly obeyed a request to be interviewed about the death of Gordon Bailey although he insisted he knew absolutely nothing about it. He was accompanied by a senior member of the Storm's backroom staff.

Davies and West had sorted out their interview strategy which involved getting Eliot to open up about coming to play basketball in England before grilling him about his relationship with Bailey.

They were just about to go through the interview room door when a breathless Tilly Johnson chased after them.

'Boss, wait.'

'Not now, Tilly.'

'But boss, you need to see this. It's a report about an incident involving Eliot in the States.'

She handed over a file that contained a few typewritten sheets and a couple of newspaper articles.

'Sorry to be offhand with you, Tilly. I'll make sure I have a good look at it while we're in there. Thank you.'

Davies and West sat opposite Eliot who appeared tense and out of his comfort zone. So different from how he was on the basketball court, Davies thought.

'Mr Eliot: thanks for coming in,' said Davies, ignoring the file Tilly had thrust at him. 'How are things at the Storm? You've had some good results lately.'

'They're going okay.'

'It'll be a big surprise if you don't make the play-offs. And I reckon you could well challenge for the championship this year.'

Eliot straightened his huge frame, taken aback that Davies appeared to be knowledgeable about his sport. He began to relax.

'You know what our coach says? It's not where you are at the beginning or in the middle of the season that counts – it's where you are at the end.'

Davies smiled. Most coaches had a surfeit of sayings they trotted out at every opportunity: some playcallers found they were a great way of engaging with their players; others did it to make themselves sound better than they actually were. Davies believed Jason Ross was one of the former.

'And how good a coach is Mr Ross?'

'He's good, no doubt about it. Really knows his Xs and Os. England is not the hottest place for basketball and it can be difficult to build a team. But coach Ross gets the best out of his players.'

West was baffled. 'Xs and Os?'

'It's to do with tactics. Offences and defences.' Davies' knowledge impressed Eliot. 'So what's his secret?' wondered Davies.

'Spends time every day on fundamentals. He aims to maximize our strengths and cover up our weaknesses. He's definitely made me a better player – when I go out onto that court I'm determined to do my utmost for him. I believe the rest of the team are too.'

West was impatient and wanted to find out whether Eliot could have been involved in Gordon Bailey's murder. Eliot maintained he'd never met Bailey.

There was a brief lull before Davies lifted his eyes from Tilly Johnson's file.

'You're absolutely sure you've never come across Gordon Bailey before?'

'I'm certain. I just don't recognise him.'

'And how would you describe your relationship with reporters – do you get on well with them?'

'Depends. If they're okay with me, I'm okay with them.'

'But what would happen if a reporter wrote something about you that wasn't true?'

Eliot wondered where the line of questioning was going.

'It would depend on what was written. Mostly it's part of the job of being a sportsman. You take the rough with the smooth. We all like to read good things when the team's won a game, so we have to take criticism when we lose.'

Davies looked carefully at the file, stared at Eliot, then at West, then back again at Eliot.

'You didn't take the criticism from Roberto Ramirez very well, did you?'

Eliot's face tensed as he turned towards the wall and then brought his fist down hard on the table.

'Damn. I can't believe you brought that up.'

'Why wouldn't I? You seem to have a thing about getting revenge on reporters you've had an issue with.'

'First of all, Ramirez didn't write anything about me. And the police didn't take any action. Nobody could prove anything. That was because I was NOT involved.'

Davies knew he'd unsettled Eliot but there was a long way to go before the American might incriminate himself.

'All right, Mr Eliot. Tell me exactly what happened.'

The words flowed from Eliot's mouth as though he'd told the story countless times.

'I was living in California. I was going through some problems, so when an old friend invited me to spend a few days with him in Florida, I jumped at the chance. He played for a Division I school and I thought it would be good to take in a few basketball games without there being any pressure on me.

'Anyway, just before a really big game, Ramirez wrote an article claiming the school in Florida had violated NCAA rules and might be thrown out of the end-of-season tournament. Not a word of it was true.

'One night I went out for a meal with my friend and some other guys from the college. There were a couple of football players and some from the hockey team who tagged along as well. We happened to see Ramirez, so the guys confronted him. He's an asshole – he thinks he knows everything. The guys told him he'd got his facts wrong, but Ramirez reckoned his source was a good one and before too long the college would be found out.

'Well, some of the guys lost it and jumped on Ramirez. I got away as fast as I could. It was nothing to do with me – I thought I'd be in big trouble if anyone saw I was part of that group.'

Davies moved closer to Eliot and held his gaze. 'You're a big guy – you can take care of yourself. I bet loads of people are intimidated by your size and don't come near you because of that.'

He returned to the file, looking for the relevant information.

'A pity you didn't stay and help Ramirez out. Maybe you could have persuaded the group not to assault him. He had a pretty bad time by all accounts. Spent the best part of a month in hospital. Multiple bruises, lacerations, fractured eye socket – for a while the doctors thought he might have brain damage. And you say you weren't involved.

'You were going through a bad time, drugs were found in your apartment, your girlfriend pregnant – you could easily have lost control and taken out your frustrations on Ramirez.'

'Look, I've never taken drugs in my life. I like a drink – who doesn't? But on the night Ramirez was beaten up I had nothing to do with it.'

West kept up the pressure, determined to test Eliot's resolve.

'Let's look again at the night Gordon Bailey was murdered. Where were you? Can anyone vouch for you? You could have had an argument with Bailey, attacked him and returned to Derby as if nothing had happened.'

The tension was mounting as Eliot fought to get his point across. 'You've got it all wrong. I don't get violent when I've been drinking. How many times do I have to tell you – I don't know this guy Bailey. I've never set eyes on him before, so how could I have an argument with him?'

Davies decided the interview had run its course.

'Okay, Mr Eliot, that'll be all for now. We're releasing you while we continue our inquiries. Don't go leaving the country, will you? Not before the end of the basketball season anyway.'

53

It wasn't the gourmet food that attracted Davies and West to the city-centre pub, nor its 'unrivalled' range of real ales. They preferred the establishment because it was 'old-fashioned but in the best possible way'.

In one section couples were enjoying a meal together in the warm, cosy atmosphere although families with young, potentially boisterous children were threatening to ruin the ambience.

West noticed several mature women, some in small groups, others on their own, unafraid to pop in for a reviving drink after a day of retail therapy. A place worth remembering, he thought, for an evening when he was at a loose end.

They both plumped for half a pint of real ale, served straight from the jug, before settling down in a corner. On a cold evening they enjoyed the open fire which was throwing out heat across the room. They hardly noticed the oak beams, the wooden floor and anything else that might have attracted other people to the hostelry.

Davies was eager to hear about West's discreet enquiries.

'Boss, I've looked into Detective Superintendent Holland's background and it's quite interesting. He has of course listed his directorship of Eureka Homes in the force's register of interests – I'm sure if anyone tackled him about it he'd say it didn't impact on his day job. It looks as though he's been careful and not accessed the police computer system to find out anything that would benefit Eureka.

'But how about this: I've checked out Eureka at Companies House. They're making huge profits. Nothing wrong in that, although the relatives of some of the residents might think differently.

'Here's the intriguing bit: there are four main directors listed. The company chairman Geoffrey Gastrell. He's one of those guys who puts his name to all sorts of organisations and is merely a figurehead. I reckon he's a sleeping partner who doesn't have much involvement in the day-to-day running of the business.

'Apart from Keith Holland, there are two other directors: Melissa Stone, wife of MP Roger Stone. And Alan Holland, Keith's brother.'

Davies' eyes widened as he contemplated the implications of West's research.

'I bet I can guess who's really the boss. Okay then, what do we know about Alan?'

'Not a lot. Studied accountancy and finance at university. Got a job with a council, moved around a bit trying to make a name for himself, then jacked it in to become finance manage for Eureka. No criminal record, never been involved in fraud – he's clean.'

Davies had a meticulous look around to make sure no one was paying them any attention.

'Good work, James. That means Keith Holland has got to be a suspect. He could have murdered Gordon Bailey or given the word for someone to do it for him.'

'But where do we go from here, boss? You going to refer up?'

'Not at this stage. After all, what evidence have we got? No, we've got to keep this between ourselves for the time being.'

Davies finished his drink while West went to the bar for a refill. A blonde woman wearing a tight top and short skirt smiled as he looked in her direction.

Davies left, the cold air catching him by surprise. He pulled his coat more tightly around him as he went over what he knew about the murders. Could Keith Holland really have been responsible for Bailey's death? Possible although highly unlikely. But Kevin Michaels too? Davies couldn't discount it altogether – but what was Holland's motive? Something didn't make sense.

54

Hard work never fazed Tilly Johnson. She had a list of jobs to do, people to call, leads to check. She hoped that discovering Eliot's partial involvement in the assault on Ramirez had gone down well with DI Davies; she wanted her talents to be appreciated by her boss. He seemed kind, grateful even to his staff when they'd done a good job.

Her determination to succeed was matched by her single-mindedness in wanting to become a police officer, a desire she'd had since her early teens. But she'd never told anyone why she really wanted to join the force – she assumed none of her colleagues would find out.

As a girl she'd harboured an ambition to become a singer, a model or a television presenter, like most of her school friends. But that changed because of uncle John.

Uncle John.

Her father's younger brother who transformed her from an innocent girl with the world at her feet into a sullen, introverted teenager with a desire for revenge.

It started innocently enough, uncle John volunteering to keep an eye on her while her parents were out at one of the many dinners her father attended as president of the regional chamber of commerce. Uncle John said it wouldn't be a problem because when Tilly had gone to bed he could work on his laptop without being disturbed.

Uncle John.

The man her father trusted above everyone, the head of English at a private school . . . and a paedophile, attracted to girls whose purity he found intoxicating.

He started by kissing her like a close relative would – but he was unable to resist the temptation that being alone with her afforded. Before long he was going into her bedroom, doing whatever he wanted.

Uncle John.

He was the blue-eyed boy in his brother's eyes, he told her, and if she blabbed about what he'd done she'd be taken into care where even worse things would happen to her.

Her parents noticed a change in Tilly but put her mood changes down to hormones.

One night uncle John pounced on her almost immediately after her parents had gone out for the night. He hurt her so much and she cried for hours before deciding it had to stop. She steeled herself and decided to tell her mother everything that uncle John had done. She worked out how she would do it, how she had to be prepared for her mother's undoubted reaction of disbelief and scepticism.

She recalled articles she'd read in teenagers' magazines which said that if a girl was attacked there often wasn't enough evidence to convict the man who'd done it. She wanted to take a shower, to wash away the lingering aftertaste of her vile uncle – but she knew she couldn't if she was to convince her mum of what he'd done.

In her endeavours to make her parents believe her she thought about every eventuality – except one.

About midnight uncle John burst into her room and shook her awake. 'Get dressed. Something's happened to your mum and dad. They're in hospital.'

She threw on the first clothes she could find and ran downstairs. Uncle John ushered her into the cold night air, locked the door of the house behind them and sprinted to his car.

By the time they'd travelled the three miles to the hospital it was too late. Both her parents were dead, the victims of a man in his early twenties who was high on drugs. He'd stabbed them in a public car park when they refused to hand over money, jewellery or anything else he could use to buy more illegal substances.

Uncle John was just as distraught as Tilly. But the deaths of her parents made her even more determined to get away from him.

When social services were called in she told them she wanted to make a new start. She went to live twenty miles away with foster parents who loved her as their own. A new home and a new school, far enough away from uncle John to rebuild her life. But there was nothing to stop him targeting other young girls.

The grieving process took longer than she thought. With the help of understanding teachers as well as her new family she began to put her ordeal behind her. But she couldn't completely forget about it:

she suffered flashbacks several times a week and her thirst for retribution grew.

In the end she realised she had to set an example to all those young people who'd become victims: she had to report what uncle John had done to her. How could she convince others to go to the police if she hadn't done it herself?

By that time she'd developed sufficient faith in her foster parents to tell them how she'd been abused and the course of action she wanted to take. They gave her total support and accompanied Tilly to the police station.

She made a video statement and shortly afterwards uncle John was arrested and charged. Before the case came to court the police discovered other young girls who'd suffered in a similar way to Tilly. In all, uncle John faced twenty-five counts of abusing and raping young girls. Yet he pleaded not guilty to all of them; his defence was that they were impressionable young girls who wanted him to show them how grown-ups behaved sexually. They'd reported him because he wouldn't do what they asked.

His denial meant that Tilly had to go into the witness box to give evidence. Although she was terrified of the prospect, she relished it too because it meant she could reveal what a monster he was.

The jury found uncle John guilty of all the charges. He was sent to prison for twenty years, with the judge condemning him for not showing a hint of remorse for 'the most depraved and horrific campaign of sexual abuse that I've ever come across'.

Tilly put her ordeal to the back of her mind, working hard at school and gaining the qualifications she needed to join the police. Sometimes she wondered whether she ought to aim for the drugs squad so that she could prevent suppliers selling stuff to people like the man who killed her parents.

But whenever a new child sexual exploitation scandal emerged in the media – Rotherham, Rochdale, Telford – it strengthened her determination to protect young children from people like uncle John. They needed a voice and she would help them to be heard.

She knew what those youngsters were going through; if she were involved, they could never say no one believed them or they'd made up their story. In time she would apply for a transfer to child protection. Then all the uncle Johns would meet their match.

55

A uniformed officer stood sentry-like outside the front door and moved out of the way to let the investigators enter.

Davies and West didn't expect to find that Gordon Bailey lived in anything resembling a newly built showhome – but they could hardly believe their eyes when they went inside: wherever they looked they saw mountains of newspapers, thick wads of cuttings and scores of notebooks. Over his career Bailey had retained copies of every story he'd written. There were clippings of stories from other newspapers that he thought might help him with his research. And there were so many old papers and magazines that the fire service would have classed the place as a severe fire risk.

Some of the cuttings, particularly those from the early part of Bailey's career, were classified, cross-referenced and catalogued. Davies thought it was extraordinary that Bailey had been so intent on getting scoops. His meticulous filing must have been one of the reasons why he'd been successful in his career – when he'd been sober.

But it appeared that in the past few years he'd lost the inclination to maintain his comprehensive archive; there were boxes of cuttings that would never be filed in either alphabetical or chronological order.

Davies flicked through a few of the notebooks which went all the way back to when Bailey was starting out as a cub reporter. There were names that didn't mean anything to Davies as well as long, detailed passages written in shorthand which the inspector couldn't decipher. However, Bailey had methodically written the date at the start of each new day. And each notebook bore on the front cover the date on which Bailey started and finished writing in them.

There was nothing else that could be described as extraordinary anywhere else in the flat: a few clothes tossed to one side, a half-empty bottle of whisky and one glass, a couple of cartons from a nearby takeaway and pots left unwashed in the sink.

'Get someone else down here to help with bagging this lot,' Davies told West. 'We'll have to call in a shorthand expert to wade through the notebooks. And I pity the poor soul who's got to go through all those articles.'

Yandel Eliot picked up his car keys and stared at them. He hated driving, especially in England. But there were times when he had to overcome his fears and get behind the wheel. After all, he could hardly get on a bus – he wanted to remain anonymous at times like this and he couldn't do that by taking public transport. Anyway, he'd often heard people complaining about how bad the buses were – you had to change two or three times to get wherever you were going and you had to wait ages for a connection.

He ran his fingers through his hair, tapped his pocket to make sure he had his wallet, pulled his baseball cap over his forehead and left his apartment.

He enjoyed living in the former mill village of Darley Abbey, a charming, affluent area full of history and charm on the outskirts of Derby. He had Darley Park on his doorstep, a huge expanse of open space where he could chill out and look at the vast number of flowers, although he hadn't got a clue what they were called.

He could walk to the city centre from the village and it wasn't far to the main roads which could take him to all parts of the country.

The narrow streets were fairly quiet as he eased the car away from the village onto the A61 and picked up the A52 to Nottingham.

Motorists honked at him as he kept to 40mph in the inside lane in his club car, specially modified to accommodate his spindly legs which nevertheless still threatened to make contact with his chin.

Sweat was pouring down his back and chest as he reached his destination, parking in the most inconspicuous place he could find.

He walked towards an alleyway, feeling uncomfortable in the sort of area he wouldn't normally visit. It was one of the forgotten districts of Nottingham, starved of money by the city council, where a significant percentage of the residents relied on food banks and where crime had reached almost epidemic levels.

But Eliot also believed in the principle of supply and demand: he had a particular need and there was someone here who could satisfy it.

He tried to blend into the background, hoped no one could see him. Difficult, he thought, when you're as tall as I am. And not easy when there were unemployed people trying to fill their endlessly boring hours by walking the streets and stressed-out parents taking their undisciplined children home from school.

Eliot thrust his hands deeper into his pockets and kicked an empty soft drink bottle. He couldn't imagine why people would let the place they lived in become so untidy, so dirty.

'Okay, big fella?'

Eliot jumped. For a split second he was overwhelmed with fear and panic. Maybe it was a local hard nut who wanted to have a go at him simply because of his size. But then he realised who it was.

'Shit, man, don't creep up on me like that.'

He turned to face the newcomer and stared, scarcely believing what he saw. 'Gee, what's happened to you, Hayden?'

Wood's left eye was partially closed, his bottom lip was twice the size of the top one and his head was wrapped in a bandage that was tinged with blood. He had a brace on his knee and a stick helped him to keep his balance.

'A small argument that you've no need to worry about. So, have you got the money?'

'Sure. Have you got the goods?'

251

Wood smiled, checked that no one was watching and handed over the package.

56

On their way back to the office Davies decided to make a detour. The Felicity Strutt inquiry had been low on his list of priorities yet he knew Detective Superintendent Holland would be far from happy if there was no progress.

Davies drove onto an industrial estate on the edge of the city. West noticed that they passed a number of units housing everything from garages and welding equipment companies to firms specialising in waste disposal. Some kept their premises in pristine condition. Others, by the nature of their business, looked unappealing. The two men wound up their windows as pungent, nauseating smells permeated the car.

At the end of a cul-de-sac they parked outside a long, soulless building, the indoor venue of one of the county's best and most respected archery clubs.

Half a dozen people stood on a grey surface behind a yellow line. In the distance was a series of targets backed by netting.

Davies watched as one of the members composed herself, took aim and released an arrow which swished through the air. Bullseye.

'A proper Maid Marian,' West said without thinking. He regretted it as Davies gave him a stern look.

'Gentlemen, may I help you?' The gruff but friendly voice belonged to Graham Brookes, the club secretary and factotum. He'd taken early retirement from a credit reference agency and his healthy pension enabled him to dedicate his time to his passion.

He wore a dark, wool, checked herringbone jacket over a blue button-down shirt and light-coloured chinos. He'd lost most of his hair; he kept what there was at the back and sides short, visiting a barber every three weeks. His goatee beard was tidy and was trimmed every weekend.

Davies explained that he and West were making enquiries about a former member of the club, Rob Woodcock.

'Oh, him. We had to get rid of him in the end. Suspended him for "inappropriate behaviour". The committee were just about to consider his future and he tried to pre-empt the decision by resigning. But I'll say one thing about our constitution: it's as solid as a rock. A member can't just resign if there are any outstanding matters against him or her. The committee wouldn't accept his resignation, so he was unceremoniously booted out.

'That meant we could notify the other fifteen archery clubs in the county so that Woodcock couldn't try to become a member somewhere else.'

West was anxious to find out more.

'How "inappropriate" was his behaviour?'

'Well, he got a bit angry one evening. Several people thought he'd been drinking before he got here. Someone made a comment about his wife, nothing particularly offensive as far as we're aware, and he went crazy. Threatened to put an arrow in the member's chest.

'Everyone ganged up on him. That's the sort of thing that happens here. Most archery clubs in the county are a tightly-knit community and this is no exception. We managed to calm him down, put him in the office where we could keep an eye on him and sent for a taxi to take him home. Thankfully we've not seen him since.'

Davies had gone quiet. West continued the questioning.

'Do you get many people coming here who fancy themselves as Robin Hood?'

Brookes' voice took on a harsh tone. 'Of course we don't. It's a sport, something that people do as recreation. We don't let any Tom, Dick or Harry loose on the range. Do you know how fast an arrow can travel? Two hundred and twenty-five feet per second. That's a hundred and fifty miles an hour. That's why we vet potential new members very carefully. On the face of it Woodcock appeared to be the sort of person who would fit in well. Professional, working for a respected business. But we can't have people who're unable to control their temper.'

He looked West straight in the eye before continuing: 'Don't worry, we managed to sort it out among ourselves. We didn't have to call in the Sheriff of Nottingham . . .'

On the way back to the car West noticed a change in Davies. 'What's up, boss? You look as though you've seen a ghost.'

'Oh, nothing. Here, you drive.'

Davies handed over the car keys and sat in the passenger seat. He was quiet for the whole journey back to the police station. In his head he replayed the conversation he and West had had with Woodcock about Felicity.

Initially he was certain Woodcock had nothing to do with her disappearance. Now he wasn't sure. He normally took pride in being able to read people. But had he got Woodcock wrong? Had Felicity's husband hoodwinked him, pulled the wool over his eyes? Woodcock had lost control at the archery club; he could have lost his temper with Felicity too.

57

Davies' legs protested as he propelled himself forwards. His heart was thumping with the same vigour as the fully inflated basketball on the hardwood court. Beads of sweat trickled from his forehead into his eyes. His brain screamed at him: 'What the hell do you think you're doing? You're not a teenager any longer!'

It had seemed such a good idea when one of the guys in cybercrime suggested he join them for a scrimmage. Davies thought a bit of a run-out would help him to put to one side all thoughts about the murder inquiries.

The basketball team were in training for a friendly against the Met Police. Some officers looked on it as a couple of days in the capital away from nagging partners and needy kids. Others saw it as an opportunity to put one over their arrogant colleagues as well as having a few good sessions in the London pubs.

'It's all right for you,' Davies said to Danny Adamson. He was a likeable hard worker who could have played at a decent level if he hadn't put his police career first. 'You need the exercise – you're stuck behind a computer all day.'

'Yeah, but you need something to take your mind off all those criminals who're giving you the runaround. Besides, Miles, you've played the game before. You can't say that about everyone who makes up our bench.'

Even though it was a training session, Davies threw himself into it. When Adamson missed a lay-up on a fast break, Davies was the one who followed up the shot, rebounded the ball and scored under the basket.

But there was no time to celebrate. He raced back to take up a defensive stance as the opposing team's point guard took little time getting the ball over the halfway line.

Davies regarded himself as reasonably fit, able to run five or six miles without getting breathless even when he had to go up a couple of steep hills. But basketball was an entirely different proposition: one short sprint after another, bodies banging into opponents – which idiot came up with the notion that it was a non-contact sport? – and a relentless pace.

Davies suddenly had great respect for the Storm and professional clubs like them whose fitness levels were much greater than he could even think of attaining.

Five minutes later Adamson called the scrimmage to a halt. Davies stood, hands on knees, gasping for air yet trying to slow his breathing.

'Good job, Miles.' Adamson handed Davies a water bottle and he took a long swig. 'There's a place for you in the starting five against the Met if you can make it.'

'We'll see. Depends how the investigations go. Of course I'd love to play but . . .'

'Sure. I understand. See what you can do.'

Adamson made off towards the dressing room, then turned back.

'Your son's interested in basketball, isn't he? Take one of our balls. If you get a few spare minutes you might be able to get in a bit of practice with him.'

58

Davies was about to go into the first briefing of the day when his office door burst open. The face belonged to someone he really didn't want to see this early in the morning: Leyton Cook.

The professor bore even more of the traits of an eccentric than usual: thinning hair all over the place, clothes not matching properly, his beard which desperately needed a cut appearing to have creatures growing in it.

'Inspector, good to see you again. I thought you simply had to look at this, so I jumped on the first available train to come and show it to you personally.'

'There was no need. An email would have been okay. You really shouldn't have bothered.' Davies struggled to disguise the sarcasm in his voice.

'I think I owe you an apology. I've been leading you in the wrong direction.' Cook was enthusiastic rather than contrite.

Davies turned to face him, hardly believing what he heard.

'I've been studying some new research. It's in a paper about psychopaths and which jobs they're attracted to.

'Now, what I was saying about your killer being on a mission and having mental health problems is probably still correct – but I'm inclined to think he may not necessarily have a low IQ and be unemployed.

'This research says psychopathic attributes are found most commonly in business leaders and lawyers. But look at this: third on the list of jobs likely to attract a psychopath is . . . the media. And in seventh place come journalists.

'This should help you to narrow down the field somewhat. If I were you, inspector, I'd be concentrating on Gordon Bailey's colleagues. Any one of them might have a motive for murder. And if you're struggling to find the killer there, reporters on the East Midlands Express should be your next port of call.

'What else can you tell me about the victims? Were they the best reporters in their field? Do you think they trod on a few toes and got positions that someone else aspired to? Jealousy and revenge, inspector. They could be at the heart of these cases.'

Davies listened with incredulity. Cook's initial prognosis had changed completely. This was a man who was supposed to be at the forefront of new ways of working, someone who led and others followed. But Cook just seemed to accept any new ideas that came along, twisted them to his own way of thinking and claimed to be a trailblazer. He appeared unable to discern what was pioneering and what was press-release fodder designed to grab as many headlines as possible.

'Thanks for your wisdom. I'm sure my team will want to show their appreciation when they've made an arrest. If you'll forgive me, I must go – traditional, less exciting methods of policing are calling me.'

Paul Allen couldn't resist making a joke most of the time. He'd got the habit not just from his father but his uncle and elder brother too. On his nights off he could be found in one of the East Midlands' comedy clubs. He considered they were just the tonic, especially after a stressful day trying to catch criminals.

But there were certain situations that really didn't lend themselves to humour and this was one of them.

He was sitting in the same, small office at the TV station that Tilly had occupied when she was looking at Gordon Bailey's stories to see whether someone had a reason for killing him. After only two minutes he understood what DI Davies meant about not finding much to laugh about in Bailey's reports.

Allen wasn't a fan of regional television: he thought the programmes were usually too long and the producers who decided which stories to cover often ran out of ideas long before the end.

In his youth he was a middle-distance runner; now he retained an interest in athletics and was always keen to find out which local track and field competitors might make the grade. But there was nothing on regional TV to keep him entertained and the only time athletics was mentioned was if an international star was competing at one of the few prestigious events taking place in the East Midlands.

The first of Bailey's reports that Allen came across was about an organised gang involved in grooming young girls for sex. Allen tried to remain detached as the reporter revealed the shocking facts about the case. But he couldn't stop thinking about his ten-year-old daughter all through the piece.

Bailey seemed to be preoccupied with crime. Or was it that his bosses thought he could deliver crime stories in such a gripping way that he couldn't fail to keep viewers enthralled?

Allen carried on watching for the best part of an hour, becoming more and more bored with Bailey's insight into the dilemmas faced by different communities as well as regularly reporting on whether justice was being served in the courts.

There were also stories about Roger Stone, his face appearing regularly on the monitor. Perhaps too regularly, thought Allen. Stone evidently knew how to play the media: he recognised which stories would make the airwaves and knew the best time to get maximum publicity for his views – typically at weekends and bank holidays.

There were archive stories Allen expected to see, such as Stone when he was an MEP ranting in the European Parliament about plans to make bananas 'free of abnormal curvature', how diabetics could be banned from driving and how eggs couldn't be sold by the dozen.

But when Bailey's face appeared on a story about care homes, Allen perked up. He noted the date: at the time Stone was still an MEP.

'Mr Stone slammed the European Parliament for failing to do more for elderly people. He said there were programmes to help older people work longer but

Brussels should hand over more money to cater for the elderly who are in care. That would mean those who'd made a significant contribution throughout their lives to the nation's and Europe's wealth could be looked after in their time of need. A passionate speech — but some of his critics questioned whether Mr Stone had an ulterior motive in raising the question.'

59

'Where are we with the Bailey investigation?'

Davies was struggling to keep the team motivated as the inquiry was dragging on.

'We're waiting to question Roger Stone,' West said. 'He's out of the country on business.'

'And what's new with the Felicity Strutt case – are we anywhere near linking her disappearance to the murders of Michaels and Bailey?'

'No, boss, nothing.' A look of resignation appeared on West's face.

'Nothing? Surely we can't have exhausted every possible angle yet?'

The room was silent. A couple of officers fidgeted, their embarrassment at not making any progress on the investigations troubling them.

'Tilly, any suggestions?'

She thought for a moment, then her face lit up.

'What about Felicity's hairdresser?'

Davies looked bemused.

'Well, what about her hairdresser?'

'Some women reveal their deepest secrets when they're sitting in the salon and someone's making a fuss of them. There are things they wouldn't believe in telling their partner – but they'll confide in their stylist.'

'Okay, speak to Woodcock. Find out where Felicity gets her hair done. See if that gives us a new lead.'

An hour later Tilly walked into one of the most exclusive salons in Nottingham city centre. It was known for keeping abreast of the current trends as well as for being busy. You wouldn't want to be the only one in there, Tilly thought – busy doesn't necessarily mean good although you'd think something was wrong if a 'multi-award-winning establishment' had few customers.

'Good morning, madam, what can we do for you today? A trim? New style? Or do you just want to be pampered?'

The receptionist, exuberant and stylishly dressed, was a good advert for the place but just a little too animated for Tilly.

She showed her warrant card and the receptionist recoiled with amazement, wondering which of her colleagues the police could possibly be interested in. She exhaled, the relief noticeable in her eyes as Tilly told her she was investigating the disappearance of one of their clients.

'Oh, you'll want to speak to Donna. She owns the company. Felicity always asks for her – always goes out with a look of satisfaction on her face.'

Tilly's smile was as fake as the receptionist's tan. She was led past several women enjoying luxurious treatments and oblivious to everything around them as they were cosseted by their personal stylist.

Donna had just finished with one of her regulars who admired herself in the huge mirror that dominated the far end of the salon. Well worth the money, the client thought, even though her husband might have a different point of view.

Donna made sure the woman was wrapped up in her coat and had her umbrella to hand as she showed her to the door. 'Be with you in a minute,' she whispered to Tilly.

As Donna bounced back across the room Tilly took a good look at the salon owner's nonchalant, flowing, layered tresses, her loose-fitting, white blouse that was more *haute couture* than high street and her elegant black trousers that emphasized her long legs and small hips.

'We'd better go into my office,' Donna said after Tilly introduced herself.

'Coffee?'

'Please.'

Donna asked a junior to get the drinks before leading Tilly into a nondescript office with a small desk and two chairs.

'Not the most comfortable, I admit,' Donna admitted. 'I don't spend a lot of time in here. Tend to do paperwork at home. I'd sooner spend the money out there, where the clients can feel the benefit. Now, how can I help you?'

Tilly told her about the investigation into Felicity's disappearance.

'It's terrible. I hope nothing untoward has happened to her. Saw that she'd vanished. She was here that afternoon – before she went missing.'

Tilly's concentration went up a notch.

'What time was that?'

'Must have been just after two. Rang up beforehand to book an appointment. Said she'd got less than an hour and could I fit her in. I said I'd do what I could – but I knew she'd look really great afterwards. Subtle yet sophisticated – she's a classy lady, no doubt about it.'

Tilly nodded in agreement.

'How long has she been coming here?'

'Nearly two years. One of her colleagues, she's a presenter, she recommended Felicity to come here. Naturally we did a good job and she's been loyal ever since.'

Tilly sipped her coffee. It was slightly bitter but she hadn't had a drink since early that morning and it really hit the spot.

'And on that afternoon, how would you describe Felicity's mood?'

'She was on cloud nine. She's the type who always seems happy but on that occasion more so than usual. You could tell there was something different about her. There's usually a certain relationship between a stylist and her clients – what's said in the salon stays in the salon. But I don't think it's a breach of confidentiality if I tell you I think she was in love. She never said it, but her skin was glowing and her eyes sparkled.'

'And did she mention her husband?'

'Not once. I reckon there's a new man in her life. She was seeing him that evening.'

Tilly finished her coffee and stood up.

'I don't think I've spoken out of turn,' Donna said, hoping for absolution. 'I just hope you find her soon. And, by the way, if you need your hair doing, I'll book you in. I'm sure we can give you a special rate.'

60

The five-bedroomed detached house in West Bridgford looked as though it belonged to a successful businessman: it was the sort of property a banker, barrister or hedge fund manager would be delighted to call home.

The immaculate lawns were surrounded by mature trees and led up steps to a remodelled house frontage and a substantial patio. A one-year-old, top-of-the-range BMW was parked in front of a double garage.

To the side and back of the house, views over neighbouring fields would have given many potential homeowners an avaricious thrill and estate agents a guarantee of a significant profit.

As dark, menacing clouds threatened to spoil anyone's hopes of a rare, dry day, Keith Holland sent gravel flying in all directions as he hurtled up the drive. He slammed the car door shut and pulled up the collar of his classy Scandinavian raincoat as his footsteps crunched along the drive. He fidgeted after rapping on the door.

Thirty seconds later it inched open until the occupant was sure of the visitor's identity.

The man looked as though he hadn't slept. Bags under his eyes and three days of growth on his face made him look older than he was.

His hair hadn't seen a brush or a comb that morning. His crewneck sweater needed a wash while his jeans looked as though he'd been gardening in them.

'You look awful. What's going on?'

Alan Holland moved out of the way. He knew his brother wasn't keen to be seen in his company. He pointed to the kitchen.

'Coffee?'

'Not the way you make it. And I haven't got time for niceties. You know why I'm here?'

'Yes, of course. The care homes.'

'Why aren't you keeping control of everything?'

Alan's face went red as he realised that Keith's dark brown eyes, more piercing than he'd ever noticed them, were boring into him.

'These are old people we're dealing with. They die, you know.'

'Well, if they do, make sure it's put down to natural causes. And don't let the staff get out of line. If you've got any doubts about them, get rid of them. We can't afford to take any chances.'

Palms sweating, Alan began to shake; he'd never been good at handling stress.

'It's all right for you – you don't have to put up with all this. And the press have been sniffing round. I don't know if I can take much more.'

271

Keith put his arm on his brother's shoulder but Alan couldn't feel any warmth in the gesture.

'Keep your nerve. Don't make any comment to the press. We'll get through this. Don't forget, I can always pull a few strings. What I'm concerned about at the moment is damage limitation. In a couple of years people will be falling over themselves to buy us out. We'll look back on this and laugh about it, you mark my words.'

Alan's expression indicated he wasn't convinced.

'Some of your minions have been asking questions since that old woman died. You don't have any idea how much shit we could be in. And I'll be the one who's going to prison.'

'Relax, it's not going to come to that.'

'How can you be so sure?'

Keith Holland pulled his brother in closer. 'Do you think I'd ever let anything like that happen to you? We're family. Blood's thicker than water. Anyway, charges of corporate manslaughter are extremely rare. The most they can probably do us for is health and safety offences. You shouldn't go down for those.'

61

She was crawling, the exertion making her knees sore as her progress was slow and deliberate. Too slow really. She couldn't wait to get out of this dark, narrow passage to find some air that didn't have a fusty, dank tang.

She heard something behind her – the tunnel collapsing. She glanced over her shoulder as the impenetrable cloud of dust headed her way and forced her to go faster. She scrambled to her feet, realising that she could now just about stand up and run away.

She gasped, a sense of being suffocated refusing to go away. Keep calm, she told herself, resume control. But how could she when she could see no way out of her predicament?

Up ahead, a light. It got brighter as she moved towards it, then shiny, radiant, dazzling as a wave of optimism engulfed her.

She hesitated, a friend's quip popping into her head: 'there's a light at the end of a tunnel but it could be a train coming the other way!'

No, it can't be – this tunnel's too small for a train. She tried to resume her way towards the light but her feet wouldn't move. They were set firm, as though they were in cement. Anxiety came rushing back, along with helplessness and vulnerability.

Was this it? Would she start to see her whole life hurtling in front of her eyes until she took her last breath of this oppressive atmosphere?

She felt her legs leave the ground and her body arch backwards. Strong arms held her, the heat from the man's body sending an electrifying tingle through her.

'Let's get you out of here.' The voice with the southern American accent was masterful yet soothing at the same time.

She turned to confront her saviour and couldn't believe who she saw: George Clooney! She was glad he was supporting her, otherwise her legs might have buckled beneath her.

How could she repay him for coming to her rescue? She was contemplating the rapture to come when she heard another voice.

'It's not good for you, you know – too much sleep. It's almost as bad as not enough.'

The image of Clooney was replaced by that of her captor. Her arm throbbed with the pain of being handcuffed to the bed.

'Bad dream, was it? I had a good night's kip. Slept like a log. Never mind, you'll soon be able to sleep in your own bed again.'

He saw an astonished look on her face.

'Yes, I'll let you go soon. Just going to have some breakfast, then I'll take off the cuffs and you can go wherever you want.'

There was something about him which meant she didn't trust him, didn't believe a single word he said.

Davies and Tilly Johnson were walking out of the station at the same time when a rumbling noise emanated from Davies' stomach. 'Fancy a bite to eat? I'm starving.'

They found a corner table in a pizza restaurant a short drive away, both of them laughing as they sprinted across the car park to prevent themselves being soaked by a heavy drizzle.

Over their seafood pasta the talk turned to how their jobs could prevent couples from building lasting relationships.

Tilly paused before she dared to ask about the difficulties in Davies' marriage.

He confessed: 'I suppose the main problem was that we weren't true to each other.'

'How do you mean?'

'Well, when you first get together with someone, the pair of you make allowances for each other – there's plenty of give and take. You'll go along with anything the other person suggests. But there comes a time when something happens and you react in a way the other person doesn't expect. You're always trying to keep the other person happy. By the time you show your real self, it's too late – marriage and children have got in the way and one of you feels trapped.'

Tilly kept her eyes on her plate. 'Did you feel trapped?'

Davies swallowed a mouthful of garlic bread and swigged from a glass of mineral water before continuing.

'Lorraine and I weren't honest with each other about what we wanted from our marriage. I suppose I was looking for a sort of utopia

275

– everything in the garden would be rosy once I'd finished work for the day.

'Lorraine was ambitious for me and encouraged me to go for promotion. She also wanted children. But when we had Jordan, she realised my job was so intense that I wasn't always there to share the responsibilities of parenthood. And she changed. She was always ranting on about one thing or another. I suppose we were as bad as each other – expecting something that wasn't there. The sad thing is I'm sure Jordan will be affected somehow by our separation; I just hope he isn't too traumatised by it.'

Davies concentrated on his pasta. Tilly had already put down her cutlery after demolishing everything on her plate.

'You can tell who's been doing all the talking,' said Davies. 'What about you – ever been married? Serious relationship?'

Tilly avoided his gaze before answering.

'There was someone once.'

'Go on,' said Davies. 'Tell me all about it.'

'There's not much to tell.'

She hesitated again before continuing. There was no way she was going to reveal her troubled childhood to her boss. Not now at any rate.

'I'm not like some people who live in the past, tell everyone how unlucky they are and how life's treated them so badly. You've just got to accept what happens, learn from it and move on.'

She sipped her drink, took a deep breath and established eye contact again.

'I think I must have been at a low ebb at one point in my life because I got involved with an old family friend. We had a relationship but I realised I didn't love him.'

Davies saw the merest hint of a smile in her eyes as she carried on.

'I broke it off when I realised that if we got married, I'd become Tilly Tilley.'

62

'Boss, we've finally had the chance to look through Felicity Strutt's phone log. Nothing astonishing, apart from several calls in the week before she disappeared to one number: Chris Watson's mobile.'

West continued: 'We've also done a trawl of local taxi companies. You know Watson's a big bloke – he has to have one of those vehicles with at least five seats in it so that he's got enough room for his legs. He uses one particular cab company quite a lot. And on the night Felicity went missing he got a taxi to Mansfield Road. He was dropped off not far from the hotel – the one that was being very secretive about whether Felicity had stayed there. A couple of hours later he was picked up again, just around the corner from the hotel, and taken home.'

'Good work,' said Davies. 'Bring Watson it. He's got plenty to answer for now.'

An hour later Watson was led into the police station, his thunderous voice echoing around the building although no one was intimidated by his height nor his demeanour.

'What's all this about? You drag me from my office in front of my staff, you stick me in the back of a police car with my knees around my ears and no one will tell me anything. What's going on?'

'Ah, Mr Watson.' Davies smiled as he greeted the TV station boss and ushered him along a corridor to an interview room where James West was waiting.

'I must protest in the strongest possible terms about the way I've been treated. Who do I complain to?'

Detective Superintendent Holland, thought Davies. He loves to hobnob with 'celebrities'. But he knew Watson would soon be in no position to complain.

'Mr Watson, you haven't been totally honest with us, have you?'

Watson shifted in his seat which looked as though it might snap under his weight.

'Don't know what you mean.'

'You told us on the night Felicity disappeared you were at home with your cat. I want you to look at this photograph.'

He produced the CCTV picture of Felicity going into the hotel on Mansfield Road.

'We know that a taxi dropped you off nearby only a couple of minutes before this image was taken. You can't deny it – that's you, isn't it?'

Davies and West were astonished to see Watson burst into tears. Davies always found it uncomfortable to see a man cry, no matter how difficult the ordeal he was facing. He watched Watson's cheeks become moist and his shoulders arch forwards.

'Felicity was the love of my life,' he said eventually, 'the only woman I've ever really loved.

'She's got herself a new job with Sky. Starts in a couple of months. I'm supposed to be setting up a consultancy business. We were going away together for a holiday at the weekend. But I've not heard from her since I saw her that evening at the hotel. She's not called, sent me a text or anything.'

West, unsure whether Watson was telling the truth, wanted to know more.

'What about her husband. Did he know anything about this?'

'Of course he didn't. Hadn't got a clue. Felicity said she'd had enough of him clinging to her all the time. Couldn't wait to get away from him.'

'So how long have you been seeing her?' Davies was on the verge of believing his story but needed convincing.

Watson was beginning to compose himself. 'A few months. I invited her into my office for a chat about her future, one thing led to another, we arranged to go out for a meal and we've been together ever since.

'I haven't enjoyed all the subterfuge, the deception, hiding my feelings for her, trying to make out to the staff that there wasn't anything going on between us. I'm glad now it's out in the open. But where is she? Have you any idea?'

Davies extracted a piece of paper from a file that so far he'd not even looked at.

'Since the evening of her disappearance there've been no calls made from her phone and no activity on her bank account. In such a situation we might expect that a missing person doesn't want anyone to know where they are – but from what you've told us, we need to move the investigation in another direction.'

63

Leyton Cook sauntered into Davies' office and placed his expensive, leather shoulder bag on the desk. He looked even scruffier than the first time they met, Davies thought. Cook's hair was flying all over his head and his clothes looked crumpled as though they'd been scattered around a bedroom floor overnight.

'Now, Miles, I've been endeavouring to get into the mind of your murderer. I really can't rule out someone with a mental health problem. You're probably looking for someone with the odd conviction for assault who's finally given in to the temptation of wanting to kill. Of course he won't admit that there's anything wrong with him, so he won't be on any medication. I suggest the best thing to do is to find out how many people living within a couple of miles of the murder scenes have a criminal record that involves violence against the person.'

Davies couldn't believe what he was hearing.

'And how many people do you think that could be? Even if we rule out all females in those areas – and there's no evidence to say a woman couldn't be the killer – we're still talking about hundreds of suspects. It's all right, I'll go through them personally – I've got nothing else to do . . .'

Cook, as stubborn as ever, refused to consider Davies' objections to his theory.

'I've studied the mind of many killers and I know how they operate. You're looking for a man who's deeply troubled, who's possibly suffered a major trauma in his developing years. He picks up a newspaper or turns on the television, sees a report of something really shocking and instead of empathising with the victims, he turns his anger and resentment on the reporter whose name is connected to the story.

'It could be that the reporter has no personal interest in the case – he's just told to cover the story by his news editor. But the killer will become fixated with the reporter and decide that he can't continue to publish distressing news – he has to die.'

Davies bit his lip as he ushered Cook towards the door. He wanted to tell Cook what he thought of him but decided that wasn't a good idea; he knew Cook would go straight back to Detective Superintendent Holland who'd make his life even more difficult.

'Thanks, I'll bear that in mind,' Davies said. The only thing he agreed with was the fact that the murderer might be mentally unstable. But what was the killer's motive? Revenge? If so, what could Michaels and Bailey possibly have done to deserve such a brutal end to their lives?

At that moment West appeared, his face beaming like a child whose wish for an expensive birthday present had been granted. He showed Cook out.

'Boss, just taken a call from North Yorkshire Police. Wanted to compare notes. They've got a case of a radio reporter on their patch. Murdered. And here's the interesting bit: his tongue was cut out. They were wondering if we've got anything similar. They're emailing both of us the case notes.'

Davies sat down, pondering the significance of West's disclosure. 'Do me a favour, get Matt Reynolds to pop in here, will you?'

With his third coffee of the day on his desk, Davies read the email about Alan Bell, a sixty-five-year-old reporter who'd worked on local radio stations for most of his career. He'd spent many years in the East Midlands before retiring only a few months previously and moving up north.

His wife had been brought up in Scarborough and wanted to return to that part of the country to be closer to her family, especially their two grandchildren.

The Bells had settled 15 minutes further up the coast at Robin Hood's Bay. Davies knew the former fishing village which was built between two steep cliffs. Its maze of narrow streets helped it to retain its quaint attractiveness even when it was besieged by tourists.

Just before Bell retired, a three-bedroomed property came on the market, a Victorian cottage overlooking the sea and competitively priced. It was the right size to accommodate their grandchildren when they visited. There was a garden too, big enough for the youngsters to run about in and something to occupy Bell's time.

'Anything wrong, boss?' Reynolds walked slowly into Davies' office, a worried look on his face.

'Not at all. I need your knowledge of the Bible. You quoted something earlier about gouging your eye out if it bothers you. Does it say anything about why you should cut out your tongue?'

'Wow, boss, what a strange thing to ask!' He thought for a moment before continuing: 'There's plenty in the Bible about how the Lord hates a lying tongue and no human being can tame it. Let me check and I'll get back to you.'

Five minutes later he returned, books in hand, with a couple of coloured, sticky pieces of paper marking the relevant passages.

'There's a verse in Proverbs which says: "the mouth of the righteous brings forth wisdom, but the perverse tongue will be cut off".'

He opened the second Bible. 'If you want a contemporary version, it's this: "Honest people speak sensibly, but deceitful liars will be silenced." Does that help?'

'It may do. Thanks, Matt.'

Davies' mind was racing. In what way might Alan Bell have been a deceitful liar? Was there really a religious fanatic on the loose? What had these three reporters done which was so horrendous that it led to their deaths?

285

64

A broken-down lorry on the M18, a three-car prang on the A1 and driving rain held up Davies and West, so more than four hours later they arrived in Robin Hood's Bay.

They parked in a back street and walked up stone steps past a manicured lawn and trimmed borders to where Maureen Bell greeted them.

She looked younger than sixty-two. Her skin was taut and there were a few wrinkles around her green eyes which still sparkled even though she'd been crying. Her clothes were classy without being gaudy, fitting her trim figure perfectly.

Davies lowered his voice as he apologised for having to go over the details of her husband's demise again even though the North Yorkshire officers had produced a comprehensive report into Bell's murder.

Maureen was almost dispassionate as she answered one question after another. But she became surprised when Davies wanted to delve into Bell's background.

'Was Alan religious at all?' The question startled West as well.

'Why do you want to know that?' Her tone was unable to hide her indignation.

'No particular reason. I just wondered whether he attended church regularly.'

'Christenings, funerals and weddings. Apart from that, he never went inside a church. Said he'd committed too many sins for God to forgive him. But he was a good man. He'd never consciously hurt anybody.'

Davies had got to the point he was dreading – the reason why they'd travelled a hundred and thirty-odd miles to the coast.

'I'm sorry to have to bring this up, but do you think there's any significance in the fact that Alan's tongue was cut out?'

It was as if Davies had switched on a tap. Maureen's eyes filled up, tears flowed and she clammed up.

A minute later West started to get up, his dismissive glance indicating he thought the interview was over. Davies put his hand on the detective sergeant's arm as Maureen's wailing became quieter.

'Thanks for all your help, Maureen. I'd like to ask just one more question: how was Alan's health generally?'

She swallowed hard and took a deep breath. 'He was in good shape for a man of his age. Apart from his hearing, of course.'

'His hearing?'

'That's right. Said it didn't affect him at work – he could always turn the speakers up to hear interviews and so on. But when he was at home I often had to repeat myself. Sometimes I'd have to say the same thing three times before he heard me. I told him he should go and get his ears seen to. You can get really small hearing aids these days on the National Health. He was the typical man – said he couldn't hear me because he was concentrating on something else. Was in his own little world. But I knew different.'

Davies got to his feet, thanked Maureen again and said he and West would see themselves out.

'Oh, one last thing. Did Alan ever admit that his hearing had let him down at work? I suppose there were times when he was out of the office and he might not have been able to hear as well as he needed to.'

'Well, he did come home one day complaining about the acoustics in court. He'd been to some big case and reckoned one of the barristers had the quietest voice he'd ever heard. Alan said the man shouldn't be allowed to practise if he couldn't speak up. I told him again that he should go to the doctor's. But he just brushed it off and said everyone had problems hearing what went on in that courtroom.'

65

They hadn't even got as far as the B1447 taking them out of Robin Hood's Bay before Davies was on the phone.

'Tilly, I want you to do some digging: go through any reports filed by Kevin Michaels, Gordon Bailey and Alan Bell when they've all reported on the same story. It might not be as big a job as you think. Bailey had no interest in sport, so that narrows it down a bit. Start with court cases. Bell was hard of hearing. I've just got the feeling that he might unknowingly have brought his death on himself.'

Black clouds dumped their contents on the two-lane road in front of them. West slowed down as the windscreen wipers even at double speed struggled to cope with the deluge.

'James, don't bother driving back to the office. Go straight to the East Midlands Express. Someone should still be there – if this rain doesn't wash us away down the A1.'

After the briefest of stops on the motorway for coffee and an unappealing sandwich, the two detectives arrived at the Express building. Reception had closed, so they pressed a buzzer and were eventually allowed inside.

A dishevelled reporter took them to the newsroom which was still busy. Bill Cooper was issuing orders and journalists looked frantic, dialling memorised phone numbers as they tried to stand up the latest revelations on social media.

'Looks like there's been a fatal accident on the M1. Southbound, near Milton Keynes. We think a local family's involved. We're on top of it now. All the calls are in – we're waiting for confirmation that it's someone from our patch. Now, can I help you?'

Davies looked at the reporters and realised the similarity between police officers and journalists. They all wanted to establish what happened, when, why and how. The only difference was that the police went further to determine whether a crime had been committed and who was at fault.

'We've just been to see Maureen Bell.'

'Terrible case,' said Cooper, offering his two visitors a seat. 'Met him a couple of times. A decent bloke.'

A nearby phone rang. A reporter's arm flew across the desk before he barked: 'Express newsdesk.'

Davies ignored all the noises going on in the background.

'I don't know about the ethics of this, but do journalists share information?'

Cooper composed himself, unsure where the question was leading.

'If one of our journalists unearthed a good story and passed it on to any of our competitors, he'd be out of the door. Straightaway. It's a sackable offence. Company policy.

'But I don't think anyone here would be daft enough to do that. They might flog it to one of the nationals to make themselves a bit on the side – but only after we've printed it.'

West butted in: 'If it were me, I'd be selling stuff to the national papers all the time. I bet they pay decent money for a good story.'

Cooper sighed. 'Sell a story to *The Sun* and you'll get a few hundred quid for it. Especially if you don't offer it to anyone else. But there are news agencies who are firing stuff off to the nationals all the time. They don't even check their facts before doing it. You couldn't compete with them and work full time as well.'

'Are there any instances in which reporters might collaborate?' Davies asked. 'For instance, would Kevin Michaels have worked with Alan Bell or Gordon Bailey on any stories?'

Cooper held out his hands with the palms facing Davies. 'You know what it's like to be short of staff – you can't be in two places at once. Sometimes we haven't got the manpower to send two people to court, even when there are a couple of really juicy cases. It could be that the verdicts come through at the same time. On a day like that, Kevin might have covered one case and Alan or Gordon the other. Then they'd swop details afterwards. We wouldn't condone it – but if it meant we got coverage of both cases, nothing more would be said.'

66

At the following morning's briefing Tilly Johnson produced a file containing newspaper clippings along with radio and television scripts. The room went silent.

'Michaels, Bailey and Bell have only worked on the same four stories over the past six months: the rape of a nineteen-year-old student on her way back to her accommodation in Nottingham city centre; the murder of an Iraqi woman in Derby – a victim of what was said to be an honour killing; a businessman jailed for fraud – he conned elderly people, charged them ten times the going rate for mobility scooters; and a drug dealer who was in court for sentencing for having a network of cannabis farms across Nottinghamshire. The last two are particularly interesting.'

She waited, eager to ensure that everyone in the room noted the significance.

'They're the only ones that overlap, as far as dates are concerned. All the media outlets published the story about the conmen on the day of the court case and saved the piece about the drug dealer until the following morning. I'll speak to the court office as soon as they open and get the transcripts sent over.'

Davies jumped to his feet. But before he could speak a voice chimed up: 'Hang on a minute!'

Paul Allen loosened his tie and cleared his throat. For once he looked deadly serious.

'A mate of mine's in the drugs squad. He worked on that case.' He turned to Tilly. 'What was the name of the defendant? Was it . . . Gavin Thompson?'

Tilly looked down at the file before nodding.

'Bloody hell! We'd better watch our step if the Thompson family are involved.'

Murmurs broke out around the room, forcing Davies to restore order.

'All right, calm down. For those of you new to the area and don't know the Thompsons, they've been a thorn in our side for a number of years. If you cast your mind back, they were one of the reasons why this city was nicknamed Shottingham.

'A lot of people have worked really hard to get guns off our streets and finger the Thompsons' collars. But they still think they're running this city. The Chief Constable thought it was a major coup when Gavin got sent down, but his older brother Ken is the driving force. I wouldn't put it past him to be behind these three killings. But at the moment I haven't got a clue about the motivation.'

He thanked Tilly for her work. Several of his team didn't fail to notice the admiration and respect in his voice.

Excitement cranked up in the incident room when the court papers of Gavin Thompson's trial arrived.

Davies was swept along by the exhilaration even though he knew he needed to be as dispassionate as possible. Keep a cool head, he thought; set the team a good example.

'All right, everyone. Let's be objective about this. We're going to read through the transcripts and check them against the reports prepared by Michaels, Bailey and Alan Bell.

'Remember, there was a huge amount of evidence at the trial and the reporters had to condense it into a short piece for the airwaves or their newspaper. Did they get something wrong? Journalists are supposed to be accurate; did they fall short of their usual standards? Did they publish something that wasn't said in court? Can we find out why someone was provoked so much that they murdered three people?'

The incident room was like a library as detectives concentrated on the transcripts and ploughed through the evidence which had been presented to the judge and jury over several days.

'Boss, look at this!'

Davies heard the urgency in Tilly's voice. As he moved towards her desk he noticed a gleam in her eye.

'This is after Thompson's been found guilty and his barrister is addressing the judge. Obviously he's trying to get as short a sentence as possible for his client. He's coming up with all sorts of mitigating circumstances, especially this: "Mr Thompson was under the influence of his elder brother. Their father died when they were young and Ken Thompson assumed the role of patriarch. He ruled his brother with an iron fist. My client did exactly what he was told for a number of years – through school, into adolescence and even adulthood. But then he rebelled. Your honour, he'd just had enough. He started taking cannabis, then decided to grow the drug to give to his friends".'

She could hardly contain the excitement in her voice. 'His barrister went on: "He became so good at it that he was able to set up a string of cannabis farms across Nottinghamshire. Not in itself something to be proud of and he truly shows remorse for what he did. But he became such an expert and covered his activities so well that his brother knew nothing about it until my client was arrested. Your honour, these are my client's first offences and it's my contention that this happened only because he had been in thrall to his brother. This was my client's way of striking out and trying to do something for himself. His only regret was that he got involved in something illegal, something he now realises will ensure he spends a substantial period in prison."

'Now, look at Alan Bell's report,' Tilly continued. 'There's not much about why Gavin Thompson committed these offences – but it doesn't say he was under the influence of his brother. It says he was in thrall to his *mother*.

295

'Boss, that backs up what Bell's wife told you. He could have been watching that court while the other two were reporting on other cases. Bell complained about the acoustics and said he couldn't hear properly what was going on. Quite easy in those circumstances to hear *mother* instead of *brother*.'

Paul Allen slammed the phone down and shouted a triumphant 'yes!'

Everyone turned towards him and waited for the revelation.

'Boss, something rang a bell with me. I've just been on to the advertising manager at the Express and he's confirmed my suspicions.

'Every year Ken Thompson puts a full-page advert in the paper on the day before Mothering Sunday. Talks about the importance of the mother to the family. How she always knows best.

'I'm not the only one who thinks it's strange – it's a talking point in our family every year. Ken Thompson absolutely revered his mother. She was his rock; he had no problem with letting everyone know how he felt about her. He put her on a pedestal and he encouraged other families to do the same.'

'And when those reports appeared about Gavin being led astray by his mother,' Davies concluded, 'that was the last straw for Ken Thompson. Those three journalists had to die.'

67

Davies put the phone down after speaking to the on-call firearms commander. The adrenaline made him feel as though he'd drunk several espressos one after the other. He allowed himself the semblance of a smile although he knew the firearms team would face a dangerous, potentially fatal situation. Ken Thompson had the reputation of being someone who liked to get his own way – and there were severe consequences for anyone who confronted him.

Davies also realised that he and his team wouldn't get anywhere near the action and they'd have to stay at a safe distance. He recalled television dramas he'd seen where detectives stormed into a hostile environment along with firearms officers. That might be okay for the small screen; the reality was that every measure had to be taken so that no one was put in danger unnecessarily. Apart from that, he was fond of his hearing and didn't want it damaged by a firearm going off at close range. Another detail that the television companies didn't take into account.

Robson Tobin, an intense, driven individual who was one of the force's twenty qualified drone pilots, strode into the incident room, laptop open at the latest footage he'd captured.

'Sir, have a look at this. It's Thompson's gaff. Gives you a good idea of the layout. Might come in handy.'

'Thanks. Email it to me. It might come in handy while we're at the scene.'

Minutes later an eight-strong firearms team was heading towards Thompson's home. It was followed closely by Davies driving his car as fast as he could without compromising the safety of other road users. James West sat alongside him and two detective constables were in the back seats.

Davies parked at a safe distance, behind one of the force's police dog vans which showed no signs of life. All four officers got out of the car. They could hear the hum of the police helicopter which came into view, hovering like a giant dragonfly preparing to pounce on a midge or a mosquito.

In the distance mothers shouted at disobedient children; a lonely dog chained to its kennel while its owners were at work barked every few seconds.

What was going on, Davies thought. It was too quiet. Had someone tipped off Thompson? Had he already made his escape? Davies exchanged anxious looks with West. A few minutes ticked away which seemed like hours to the detectives who were itching to wrap up the case of the three murdered journalists.

In effect they were there simply to tie up the loose ends, make sure everything was done by the book, guarantee there'd be no recriminations that would mean the case file wasn't closed after all.

A few hundred yards away the firearms team were in position, waiting for a signal to pounce. They remained still, their semi-automatics at the ready, helmets toning in with their black shirts and standard-issue black trousers.

They were like guests at a surprise birthday party concealing themselves and waiting to shock a friend or relative rather than preparing to confront one of the East Midlands' most notorious criminals.

Without warning the front door flew open. Thompson emerged behind Monica the cleaner, a pistol placed against her neck.

'Back off, or she gets it!'

He whispered in her ear, the voice with a hint of tenderness although the severe tone he'd used to bellow at the police was still there.

'Sorry, Monica, I don't want you to get hurt. I really didn't want to involve you – but you're my ticket out of here. Don't worry; you'll be safe with me.'

The firearms commander barked out an order to Thompson as though he were addressing his own men.

'Drop the gun – NOW! Put your hands on your head and get down on your knees.'

Thompson remained unfazed. 'No, you listen to ME. I've already killed three people. I won't hesitate to make it four. I've got nothing to lose.

'We're going to walk up to my car, I'm going to drive out of here and you won't do anything to stop me. I guarantee I'll release Monica unhurt. But if anyone follows us, I won't hesitate to pull the trigger. Do I make myself clear?'

Undaunted, the commander remained rooted to the spot.

'Don't be a fool, Thompson. Give yourself up. Drop the gun or we fire.'

Thompson knew they wouldn't take the risk of shooting Monica so he began to inch his way towards the car, ensuring she shielded as much of his body as possible.

The commander's voice was just as strong although his men detected a note of resignation: 'Hold your fire. I repeat: hold your fire.'

68

Davies opened his laptop and accessed Tobin's email. He looked at the drone footage again. 'James, follow me.'

Davies led the way along a lane which looked as if it had been a public footpath at one stage, although it seemed to have been blocked off years ago. Perhaps someone didn't want prying eyes to find out what went on at the house.

After trampling through undergrowth saturated by continuous rain over the past few days they caught sight of the standoff in front of Thompson's property.

Davies could see Thompson and his hostage; he also noticed the firearms team were powerless to stop the killer. The inspector punched the air in frustration that Thompson might get away. They couldn't do anything reckless; the hostage's life came first.

Davies got onto his radio, keeping his voice as quiet as he could, and called the detectives waiting by his car. He told one of them his position and asked him to bring the basketball that was in the boot of his car.

Davies took the ball and waited. He calculated he was about the length of a basketball court away from Thompson. He'd scored from the halfway line in a game once – but this was totally different and the stakes were much higher.

It wasn't the type of throw that would please a coach. In reality Davies just hurled it in Thompson's direction and hoped for the best. As they say in sporting circles, it was a prayer shot.

The ball soared skywards and seemed to hang in the air longer than Michael Jordan did whenever the Chicago Bulls' legend bamboozled opposing defenders. It dropped straight onto Thompson's head, startling him and causing his arm to drop away from Monica's neck.

Seven rounds were fired off almost simultaneously. Thompson fell backwards, hitting his head on the drive. Monica emitted a spine-chilling shriek, her legs buckling underneath her as she hit the ground only yards from Thompson's lifeless body. Her physical wounds would soon heal; the emotional trauma would be long-lasting.

Davies and West both clapped their hands to their ears, the aftermath of the shots ringing inside their brains for several minutes. Worse than listening to Deep Purple while standing only a few feet away from their speakers, Davies thought. He wished he'd taken ear defenders with him.

He spluttered as the distinctive smell from the firearms drifted his way, a cross between burnt toast and the pungent tang of spent fireworks.

West threw Davies an admiring look. He'd not been to a basketball game and had never experienced a shot like Davies' successful stunner.

'Boss, is that what they call a slam dunk?'

'No, James. But I suppose you could call it a buzzer-beater.'

69

Keith Holland strolled into Davies' office, a look of satisfaction on his face although it was nothing to do with the reporters' murders being solved.

'Well, Miles, you somehow managed to pull it off. A bit unorthodox, shall we say, but in the end the right result. Perhaps all those hours at basketball weren't wasted after all.'

Davies knew instantly there'd be no word of thanks.

'A pity though that you couldn't get Thompson alive and bring him before a court. There's at least three families who wanted you to do that.

'Still, it's saved the taxpayer a lot of money keeping him in jail for all those years. And this country's prisons are in such a bad way I'm sure he'd have found a way to carry on with his criminal activities from his cell.'

Davies listened, determined not to utter any comments he might regret later.

'Well, those families have got closure,' Davies said. 'They won't have to concern themselves about whether Thompson would get what he deserved in court. And they'll never have to worry about him being released from prison and wanting further revenge.'

Holland straightened his tie although the knot looked immaculate. He knocked an almost indiscernible speck off the sleeve of his suit jacket.

'Oh, Miles, almost forgot to tell you.' Satisfaction turned to glee which engulfed his face. 'Obviously someone's impressed with the way I oversee the troops here. I'm going to be out of your hair – I've been offered a job at the Met.'

Davies seethed but didn't let Holland see his reaction. What a cheek, Davies thought. His team did all the hard work and Holland got the credit.

'Congratulations, sir. I'm sure the criminals of London won't know what's hit them.'

Holland's face transformed into the smug look that Davies knew so well and despised even more.

'Naturally I'll be having a bit of a bash before I leave so that I can say farewell properly.'

And there'll be several officers who'll be on leave or have got case work they just can't put down, Davies assumed.

'Anyway, Miles, if you fancy a move down south, let me know – I'm sure I can put in a good word for you. But I expect you'll want to stay here because it's a bit more parochial. Big murder cases aren't really your thing, are they?'

They weren't Leyton Cook's either, Davies reflected, but he knew that before long the 'expert' would get a call from Holland to help with an inquiry in the capital.

70

It was a situation Davies knew well and he didn't like what he was seeing. The Storm were losing – and losing badly. They were heading for their most comprehensive defeat of the season. But for some reason it wasn't as bad as the old days when the ball club had struggled to make an impression in British basketball's top division.

Newcastle Eagles weren't the best team in the league. Yet the Storm made them look a slick, organised outfit. Derby came out flat and the north-east club took full advantage.

Rick Parker stood out as the Storm's best player, knocking down threes and passing to an unmarked teammate on the odd occasion that Derby managed to find space under the Newcastle basket.

But every time the Eagles went down to the other end of the court they moved the ball around well, finding openings with ease. If they missed a shot they gobbled up the rebound and scored at the second attempt.

Without Yandel Eliot's imposing presence in the middle, the home team were outmuscled, outfought and outplayed.

Eliot had disappeared the night before the Newcastle game, not telling anyone where he was going or that he was quitting.

Parker took his friend's departure badly, especially as he had no inkling of what Eliot was planning. Parker thought he'd convinced Eliot he could turn to him, a loyal confidante while Eliot was in a foreign country away from family and friends. That was what hurt Parker so much: Eliot had simply packed up his belongings, dropped off his car and apartment keys at the coach's office and left.

Parker knew that Eliot would find it difficult to persuade another basketball club to sign him. The Storm would probably hang on to his registration to stop him playing anywhere else, unless they decided they didn't care what he got up to and were glad to see the back of him.

Parker was professional enough not to let his disappointment with Eliot affect his performance on court. He top-scored with 25 points and dished out half a dozen assists for the Storm – but Newcastle were able to give their younger players plenty of court time towards the end as they won by twenty points.

Heads drooped as the Derby players traipsed off the court. Parker wasn't the only one who'd be calling his agent the following morning to discuss his future.

Davies looked at Tilly and noticed her eyes were more radiant than usual.

'I suppose you've got to give Newcastle credit. They made the most of the opportunity,' he said.

'Yeah, our guys couldn't be faulted for effort. But they struggled without Eliot. Hardly surprising that their heads went down. His disappearance has cast a shadow over the whole team.

'I know a lot of people will be disappointed but, after all, it's only a game – it's not a matter of life and death.'

Davies smiled. His mind was racing: he had no idea whether he and Lorraine would get back together for Jordan's sake or if his fondness for Tilly would develop into anything stronger. He just knew that from now on he'd enjoy Storm games even more, whatever the result.

71

She stretched her tired body and rattled the handcuffs against the iron frame for the umpteenth time. As with every other occasion, her arm moved a short distance but she remained firmly shackled.

She felt weak, the lack of nutritious food now affecting her ability to think. She tried to remember how many days it was since she'd been brought to this prison.

Prison? What was it that Hamlet said to Rosencrantz and Guildenstern about Denmark being a prison? 'There is nothing good or bad, but thinking makes it so: to me it is a prison.'

She managed to recall that but why was everything else in her brain so fuzzy?

She looked down at her trousers, the expensive, fashionable material covered in urine; she'd been unable to contain herself but felt no embarrassment at her predicament. The room which hadn't been cleaned for several months stank of bodily fluids, stale beer and takeaway food. But she was unable to differentiate what the smells were; her senses had faded, just as her expectations of getting away had almost vanished.

She looked up as she heard a noise. The door flew open. Fear replaced the impassiveness that had become ingrained on her face. She could cope with the surreal surroundings she'd become accustomed to — but the unknown proved an insurmountable obstacle.

The man strode in, wiping his mouth with the sleeve of his V-neck pullover. The bobbles and the faded colour showed its age. He burped as he wiped ketchup which had dribbled onto his shirt.

He leered as his hands moved down towards the zip of his trousers.

'You know where you went wrong, don't you, Felicity? You should have replied to my email . . .'

ACKNOWLEDGEMENTS

As with *Chasing a Dream,* my book about the history of basketball in Derby, *Storm Deaths* couldn't have been written without the help of several people; I'm indebted to all of them. Apologies to anyone I've missed off.

First of all I owe a huge debt of thanks to Marcus Oldroyd who was involved from the beginning, giving advice and encouragement and ensuring that DI Miles Davies has credibility. I've seen too many television dramas in which major errors are made; Marcus ensured that no such mistakes crop up in *Storm Deaths*.

I'm also grateful to Malc Shakespeare, Superintendent Suk Verma, former police officer Rob Severn, retired Derbyshire CSI Jo Mallard and retired DI Ian "Ducky" Mallard, Andrea and Michael Marren, Phill Matthews, Neil Matthews, Dr Nigel D Chapman and Robin Miller, chaplain to the Derby Trailblazers basketball club.

Thanks also to John McNeilly, Carol and Paul Magor for their unwavering encouragement and my son Sean Durkan for the brilliant cover.

Talking of which, I'd like to show my appreciation to all the subscribers to my mailing list who took the time to vote for their favourite from a choice of four possible covers. If you want to join my mailing list, you can sign up on the front page of my website, steveorme.co.uk.

If you enjoyed *Storm Deaths* please consider leaving a review on the site where you bought the book. And please feel free to get in touch. You can do so through my website, on Twitter @SteveOrmeWriter or on Facebook – search for Steve Orme Writer.

Read on for the first chapter of the sequel, *Storm Bodies*.

STORM BODIES

1

IT WAS the smell that Dan Forsyth had never got used to – but this was like nothing he'd ever sniffed before.

He wasn't bothered by the muck, the dust and the thought of what people might have put in their dustbins. It was a dirty job, yes – but someone had to do it.

He'd been doing it for eighteen years now, lugging bins up and down the street, making sure they were emptied properly, returning them to their rightful owners and putting up with barbed comments from self-centred people who weren't satisfied with the service the council provided.

Straight after a shift he'd have a shower, wash his hair and change his clothes. Initially he'd done it merely to pacify his wife; now he did it because he needed to feel refreshed. He enjoyed seeing the grime that had engulfed him during the day as it washed down the plughole.

But as soon as he was back at the depot the following morning, the smell returned as strong as ever.

He'd tried everything to get rid of it: he'd started the day wearing a surgical mask only to discard it after a few minutes because his glasses steamed up; he'd risked being the butt of his colleagues' jokes by turning up one morning reeking of a costly aftershave; and on one occasion he'd gone to work with a raging hangover after several pints and whisky chasers during a prolonged pub crawl. But still the smell wouldn't go away.

He'd contemplated making an appointment with his GP. But all his doctor would probably say was 'you've got sensitive nostrils. Live with it.'

It wasn't as if he had the enhanced smell of a superhero. He couldn't detect whether anyone was lying or if someone had a tumour simply because of the aroma they gave off.

He just happened to be the first to notice when an unusual or a particularly pungent smell was in the air.

He didn't expect anything out of the ordinary when the refuse lorry pulled into a nondescript street of Victorian terraced houses. The bins were all in their proper place, lined up on the edge of the pavement, waiting to disgorge their contents into the truck.

He was rushing around more quickly than usual as big spots of rain began to fall, forcing him to zip up his council-issue waterproof even though it didn't keep him completely dry.

He almost didn't notice a black, battered, extra-large suitcase. Dan knew it was the council's policy not to take anything that didn't fit inside a bin – but he preferred to use common sense rather than stick to the rules.

The suitcase was outside number 11, the home of Violet Campbell, a frail, harmless spinster who was well into her seventies. He thought it might have been a long time since she went travelling; and why would she need such a large case?

'Hey, Dan, shall we chuck it in the lorry?' one of his colleagues shouted.

'Yeah, can't do any harm. She's a sweet old lady. Probably hasn't got anyone to take it to the tip for her.'

But the closer Dan got to the case the more anxious he became as his nostrils picked up a smell like nothing he'd come across before. A cross between rotting fruit and raw sewage with a hint of a budget-priced perfume. He began to retch, the sickening odour lingering in his mouth and throat as well as sticking to his nasal hair.

He covered his nose with his sleeve but it made little difference. The stench grew even more sour and acerbic, forcing Dan to reconsider whether he should bother with the case. But if Violet wanted it taking away, how could he not be a good Samaritan?

He grabbed the handle and lifted. It took him most of his not inconsiderable strength to get the case off the floor.

'Bloody hell! Has she got a body in here?'

Printed in Great Britain
by Amazon